Sean Daniel was born in Cork, Ireland, in 1990, the youngest of three children. He has an honours BSc. in Biomedical Science but writing has always been his passion and true love.

He is also a long-distance runner and a long-distance traveller. He strongly believes in the value of meeting all kinds of people from all parts of the planet, believing nothing broadens his horizons like a conversation with someone different from himself.

But it doesn't have to be all go – happiness for him can be found in the form of a good book and a cup of tea, with his dogs snoozing at his feet.

Men on Earth

SEAN DANIEL

Men on Earth

Vanguard Press

VANGUARD PAPERBACK

© Copyright 2015
Sean Daniel

A CIP catalogue record for this title is
available from the British Library.

ISBN 978 1 84386 957 3

Vanguard Press is an imprint of
Pegasus Elliot Mackenzie Publishers Ltd.
www.pegasuspublishers.com

First Published in 2015

Vanguard Press
Sheraton House Castle Park
Cambridge England

Printed & Bound in Great Britain

For my loving parents, Kay and Gerard

Acknowledgements

I have little doubt that this book would not exist were it not for the support of my family: my parents Kay and Gerard, my sister Niamh and my brother Gearoid, whom I love with all my heart.

The everyday of life is ordinary, it is difficult and it can be lonely. But there is greatness in people, even when they do not know it of themselves. Never underestimate the power of belief nor the far-reaching arms of support for they move more than mountains. Such things can move minds and change lives.

And so to my friends Adam Clooney, Stephen Power, Emma Speight and Stefanie Preissner, I extend more gratitude than words can articulate. Thank you for being the main characters in my story, you make every page an adventure and every word an inspiration.

"Hell

Is Not A

Punishment.

It

Is

Earned."

CONTENTS

CHAPTER I

GENESIS

There is no escaping the gravity of this planet. It has a curious and sinister hunger for all men, created equal or otherwise. For all their powers and all their strengths, men are at mercies far beyond their control. There is a magnetism that pulls on the hopes of man. For them, there is only the great delusion, the pantomime of choice. Just as it is slow for some and quick for others, so too is it inevitable for all.

***

Perhaps he was lost, who knows, maybe even lost in the clouds. The very heavens above were restless and those below were forced to deal with the consequences. Some love a stormy night, they say that there is no other time that they feel as comfortable as when wrapped up during a storm. Comfort is something that is very much dependant on what side of the glass you happen to be on. John was lucky enough to be on the right side of the glass. But despite being on the right side of the storm, he was on the wrong side of the clock, which had been making faces at him for quite some time.

The winds wailed as the clouds clashed above, not unusual for Cork city, but not desirable either. John rolled away from the clock and window in time. He sighed at the far wall, where the orange hue of the street lamp was casting shadows great and small through the broken, slanted blinds that adorned the tall loft windows. John found the orange light of the burning, solitary, sodium street lamp comforting. It kept away the pitch of the night yet still allowed darkness. Most of all, he liked it because it was one thing above all else; it was constant. People are funny creatures; it is amazing how much faith human kind have in things that are constant. It often does not matter if they are very good things or not, just as long as they are dependable and predictable. When you really think about, what did that lamp ever really do for John? Nothing. Yet still, the fact it was there, night after night was comforting to him. Sometimes people seem to forget that you once hated a thing if it manages to stay around for long enough. More often than not you end up depending on it, it can even become comforting. But as already stated, comfort really does depend on what side of the glass you're on.

The far wall was getting wavier, streaks of ghosts from the outside world ran from ceiling to floor as the ever increasing rain bore a puppet show across John's room with the help of the street lamp. He looked at the clock, which had crept past the four a.m. mark. Then something that was unusual for this city; thunder. And not just regular thunder, but thunder that seemed to rattle the windows and shake the lights from the wall. John didn't notice, he didn't have the presence of mind nor the interest, but there was something different about these explosions of the sky. As trouble formed beneath the troposphere, he rolled flat on his back to face the ceiling and ran his hands through his hair. Despite being a relatively young man, in his late twenties, he didn't have very much going for him in the looks department. He wasn't ringing any bell towers just yet, but was by no means a Monet for the bathroom wall. As his hands fell from his head the sky above began to let loose.

That was when John began to take notice. The thunder seemed to him like it was all out of time. There was no real delay between the bangs; the bursts of air were falling all atop each other. It sounded more like someone was shelling the sky. The window was resisting assault from the rain, with droplets so fat that they sounded more like solids. At times, the thunder was so frequent that there was no gap in explosions for times upwards of minutes. But that wasn't what really grabbed John from his a.m. bed rolling. The far wall was orange. But it was only orange, all the time, without a sliver of blue. Not a trickle, not a flash. The sky was splitting, but where was the lightning? And then came the realisation that drew his eyes wide; if there really was no lightning, then what was making the thunder?

John was having one of those moments where he thought that his confusion was due to his groggy state at this un-godly hour and that maybe there was lightning. Maybe he was so over tired that he was imagining the sky without it. He thought that perhaps his window might be at the wrong angle. He sat upright on the bed with feet to the floor. The thunder had not yet relented, if anything it was worse. As he looked through the pane and squinted past the orange hue, he saw clouds so dense he thought they may crush the very rooftops. His view was less Rivera and more economy in a bad hotel. He could see the sky only at an angle; the apartment across the way was almost in reaching distance. But there, at the end of the short alleyway that lay parade to his home, sat a sky, which crept around and above the buildings. Irrespective of how loud a sky it was, it was most definitely a dark one. He could only see a sliver of the outside world, but such a thing can be precious.

Then, like a music reel creeping into a movie scene, a whistle started to build somewhere in the dark. Not a whistle from tin nor lips, but one that was being made by the wind. The rain grew thicker and thicker as the whistle increased in amplitude. It sounded like something careering though the sky, like an object entering the atmosphere. It grew louder and louder, dampened only by the thunder that wrestled with it above. John didn't know if the sound was real or if his ears had just gone off frequency. Perhaps they had begun to trick him in the way that one can hear things that are not there to be heard, especially in the dark sky hours.

Sure, I've been hearing the thunder fine all night, thought John. Then the idea crept into his head; maybe he wasn't hearing the thunder? After all, there was no lightening to be seen. The whistling grew louder as John grew less and less sure. He was all of a sudden nervous, almost frightened and what startled him more was that he didn't know why.

He plunged fingers into ears and twisted, he even started mumbling and talking out loud. The clouds roared and the whistling was now deafening. John spoke aloud to test if it was his ears that were failing him or if it was his mind.

"I'm just seeing, I'm JUST SEEING IF I CAN HEAR, CAN HEAR MYSELF!" shouted John to an empty room.

As he stood there, shouting past his reflection in the window, there was a ruptures explosion in the sky. It came from the darkest clouds in the distance, and from these clouds, a wave of light burst from every sinew and ran across the sky. This silenced the whistling and John alike. There was silence in the apartment and across the city beneath. The light reassured John of the lightening and of his sanity. But the calm of the expected, the comfort of the constant was short lived.

The whistling started again but this time it was different. The pitch or perhaps the frequency, John wasn't sure, but something, something was amiss about it. This wasn't just the howling wind, this was something different. He leaned against the window, the cold of the glass made his chest contract and his breath fog up his view. He wiped his hand across the condensation and looked out into the night in search of this ever-increasing howl. It was so intense that he had that feeling of inexplicable fear trapped in his heartbeat, the kind you can hear deep inside your ears. Louder and more shrill, the intensity of the whistle grew, it sounded like a bomb was dropping above and soon it would be down with him and the rest of the city below. His heart raced in tune with his eyes across the sky, desperately searching for the source. That was when John noticed it.

At first he thought it was his imagination, but he soon cleared that away. He knew he wasn't drunk; he hadn't had a drink in hours. Whatever the cause, it wasn't John. As he looked out the window, the storm was getting slower. Not the intensity, the actual speed. The storm was slowing down. The rain was falling slower to the earth, not in an uncontrolled manner, it wasn't the wind heaping it up or down, but instead the very droplets themselves were losing their momentum. As the whistling grew and sounded nearer than ever John put his hand against the glass and held his breath as he watched the last of the droplets explode against the frames, they glistened in slow motion. Moments later the rain had quite literally ground to a halt. He was no longer frightened; he was far past the point of fear and lost instead in mystery. He cracked open the window. As it slid upwards not a single drop entered his bedroom. Not one. The whistling was still screaming sharply in the background but faded to a dull haze as his ears had shut it out. All of his focus was on his hand as he swished it through the air outside.

He watched as he burst the mid air droplets into a fine spray. The disturbed rain stayed stationary in harmony with the rest of the sky. John's ears came back into function as he listened. He listened past the screaming of the dark and tried to focus his ears on the sound of trickling water. Nothing. There was no flowing water in the grates, no precipitation in the pipes. The air was still and the breeze was motionless. The only sound he heard was the fizz and buzz of electricity from the street lamp in unison with the whistling. The electric buzz of the streetlamp began to intensify and become louder, soon it was vibrating in deafening harmony with the whistling from above. The buzz grew until the 'clink' and flash of the bursting bulb left John and his back wall alone in the dark. At the time the streetlamp went out there was silence all about the city, just as the whistling stopped dead and sudden. No buzz, no whistle, not a hush of wind or lull from the clouds. Just silence and darkness.

Then came a thunderous boom from the darkest cloud in the distance. In a flash of nature and universe, the whistle returned and became violent as the painted world outside was kick started back to life. The crack in the sky heralded the rain to flow freely and a sheet of water came down across the city as though it had been building up above while the world below was on standby. The whistling finally stopped. It stopped at the exact moment that John's roof was breached.

The noise of shattered slates and thrashed timber filled the air as something heavy crashed though his ceiling! In the adrenaline slow motion of the situation, John saw a man amidst the debris as he broke his fall, with half his body shearing through the wooden chest of drawers. The man struck the floor like a hammer of thunder. The vibrations split the floorboards all the way across to John's feet as they ran up and into his very bones. John was no longer alone.

***

As the dust settled inside, the weather settled outside. Like the monsoon season, the rain stopped in a matter of seconds. But John had little concern with forecasts. No, instead he was more preoccupied by the dead man currently lodging with him and the gaping hole he left in the ceiling. John didn't often have guests, but when he did, they tended to use the front door. The ceiling bulb was swaying from side to side and the wires, usually hidden behind plaster, were now exposed. John did not live in the top apartment. There was one more above him, it was unoccupied and had been for some time. The left over rainwater from the roof was trickling down through the upstairs apartment and into his room making a 'plop-plop-plop' sound as it bounced off the wooden debris. The room itself was in complete disarray. The chest of drawers was decimated and the bottom right leg of the bed was in splinters.

What had just happened and where did this man come from? More pressing still was what to do with this sopping, skydive lesson-skimping, corpse on his floor? Still frozen and stiff, John could hear his own wrist joints glide as his body began to loosen, whatever he was going to do, he was going to have to get a move on. Just at that moment the body on the floor began to rustle in the wreckage. The body was not so dead after all.

"JESUS, MARY AND JOSEPH! What the fuck?" shouted John as he loosened in a flash and fell backwards over his nightstand. "What the bleeding feck do ya think you're doing, boy?! Huh!? What's this like, hah?" Trying to sound tough, John's voice was quivering in terror as the skyward silhouette began to stand before him. In fact, the only bit of courage in his voice came from the fact that he was so intensely pissed off about his ceiling.

"I, I, I, don't want any trouble, lad. I just, Jesus, are you all right, like? Did you mean to... ah seriously, buddy, I was just trying to get some fecking sleep, like."

The stranger began to stand up in the darkness and from the frame before him John could tell it was a man. As his mind was trying to process how someone could survive coming through a roof like that, John once again heard a faint buzzing sound. It was the streetlamp outside. Instinctively he turned his head towards it. 'Zz-zzzzz-clink, clink-clink' and the orange light was alive once more. As he turned his head back to the stranger, his shape had come alive as a black shadow on the back wall.

"Holy Christ, what the hell do ya think you're playing at, boy! Haa?" Slumped on the floor, John pushed back hard against the radiator until he was standing upright. "What the hell are ya doing? Huh, have you any manners, like? You can't come crashing into someone's room in the middle of the night, lad!" John was on the offensive, half fuelled by sheer adrenaline, half from utter anxiety. The stranger stood there in a motionless, catatonic state. He said nor did nothing. His lack of response was making John ever more nervous. "Look, buddy, I hope you're all right and everything but, like, I don't want any trouble okay, so just… just get the fuck out of my house, will ya?"

There was silence still from the somber stranger. The tension was pensive, John felt cornered in the room. He was beyond shock and fear and had moved into paralytic terror. "Ahh, come on, lad, what do you want from me? I don't have any money like, sure look at the state of the place? If anything, like, you made it better, ha? Ja'know what I mean ha?" The halfhearted joke was no means of hiding his fear. Still, the orange shadow of the stranger stood motionless.

John began to look closer at the stranger, he could clearly see the outline of his uninvited guest. He stood colossal across the room and he still did not stand fully. But while he stared, he noticed that there was quite a lot of steam coming off of the stranger's bare shoulders. He could see the heat waves rising against the silhouette. There was something very odd about this situation indeed. The silly thoughts and illusions of heat waves distracted John from the problem at hand – the stranger who, as far as John knew, was thinking up various ways of murdering him.

"Okay, okay. Right, lad, look, I don't know whatcha want, right? I don't know what to tell ya, like? Ah, Jesus, look at the hole you made like! Just take what you want and go okay? Do whatever it is you're here to do, like! Are you even listening to me, can you hear me?"

"Yes, I can hear you perfectly." As plain as that, a strong voice, hushed, low in volume, spoke to John calmly from the dark. "I apologise but I do not understand what you are asking of me, sir." The stranger's voice was unlike any John had ever heard, it was without accent and was sincerely genuine. John was speechless. As the two men stared at each other through the dark, the stranger spoke once again. "Forgive me, sir, but I do not understand what it is I am meant to 'take' from you and, with complete trueness, I know not why I am here. Can you tell me where here is?" There was a softness in his voice that was almost hypnotic, it made John feel warm as he spoke.

John no longer felt as threatened, despite the fact that there was still a meteorite of a man standing between him and the door. There was something about his voice that made John feel unusually safe around this stranger. Once, John's bike had been stolen from him – while he was still riding it in fact. The gang of fellas who took it were from the north side of the city, now those were accents that would strike the fear of God into you. But not this one. Stunned by the sincerity of the question from the voice that sauntered through the silence, John felt compelled to answer.

"You're in the city, boy, Cork city that is. And if you want to be more specific you're in my bedroom on Bandon Road, if that helps. I don't mean to be rude, lad, but can you tell me what in the fuck is going on? Like, where did you come from and how did you come through the roof like that?"

Again, the room was filled by a pensive pause, which evolved into awkward silence and then into tension. The lack of a reply was making John nervous once more. Finally, the calming voice gave an unreassuringly empty answer.

"I apologise but I am unable to answer your questions, sir. I only remember waking up on your floor just those few moments ago."

The voice once again brought John back down from his heightened level of anxiety, but the answer wasn't enough, not for a water soaked, crack filled floor and a four a.m. crash landing.

"Well, look, you're going to have to leave, buddy." The rush of adrenaline John experienced as he stood up to the stranger was soon replaced with a voice in his head that screamed, *No, you fool! The roof! The roof! You can't make him leave without paying for the roof!*"

It is curious, how so many thoughts try to be processed and heard all at once. There was no need for the rush of penny-pinching thought, as the stranger had not budged an inch, nor had he any intention to do so. Once more, they were both in near silence, company kept only by dripping floorboards. In the lull of the moment, John now felt his confidence return. He noticed the cord leading to his bedside table lamp, which now sat on its side as a result of the commotion. He reached slowly for the switch attached to the cord, all the while keeping his focus and eyes on the stranger. His hand crept along the wire until he felt the case and just as his thumb rested on the button he stopped. "Now, things are just a little mad, all right, lad? And being in the dark ain't helping things. So I'm just going to turn on a light, okay?" Again, his ears were met only by drops on the wooden floor. "So, like I said, just... just turning on the switch is all." With a subtle 'click' the room was lit from a sideways cone that revealed a body that John was not expecting.

The stranger was a statuesque specimen of a man, chiseled in features and dense in muscle. He was also completely naked. A mixed wave of reactions was sweeping over John at this point. In one respect, he was in awe of this man, while at the same time he was finding the awkwardness of a strange naked man almost unbearable. The stranger was extremely well built, his arms looked like those of a bare chimpanzee, massive in flesh and muscle, every sinew lined with strips of muscle and wrapped in coursing veins. However, his physique is not offensive, not protruding like the images of body builders. There was simply an air of power radiating from him. His chest followed suit; large, shapely pecks that sat above an iron clad stomach that was flanked by pellets of leaded muscle. The legs that carried him so high from the ground looked like those of an Olympic athlete in full sprint, despite being in a relaxed state. In the flash of a photon, John suddenly felt completely inferior to the stranger and the possibility of a struggle now seemed impossible to him.

For all intents and purposes, this man was conjuring images of renaissance paintings in John's head. His face was a canvas for creation. It was firm and well defined, with all features in near perfect shape and orientation, it was a strong, proud face. Yet at the same time, it was one that was welcoming, despite the animal that stood before John, his face made him seem less threatening and ever so approachable. He had thick golden locks of hair that spun like golden gossamer onto his shoulders and startling blue eyes. In fact, John noticed his eyes more than anything else. In lieu of the dim light source, the stranger was squinting, and squinting quite a bit. He nearly looked to be in pain, as though this was the first time he was using his eyes for a long time. Perhaps for the first time.

But of all the features before him, there was one that kept John speechless. It was not the statuesque body, it was not the piercing blue eyes nor was it the fact that a stranger's bare penis was just a few feet from him. No, all of these seemed to pale in comparison in the shadow of the stranger's most defining feature; the wings that were growing out of his back.

The silence mounted, second after second a new sheet was lain, each one heavier than the last until John felt so much pressure in the room he could scarcely breath. Then, those sheets shattered all around him as he spoke.

"What the bloody hell are those yokes?!" John pointed at the stranger with an out stretched finger that quivered more than his voice. "I mean it, buddy, what in the fuck is going on here?! Are those wings on your back? Wings? Wings like, growing off ya?! Take those things off... take... they're real. Are they real? What am I saying?" John paused and an unexplained composure took over.

"Are... are those really wings, lad?"

With eyes that looked as though they were becoming focused he looked John in the eye and calmly said, in a friendly manner, "Yes, these are my wings."

John wasn't quite sure what to make of that answer. The stranger said it in such a way that a person would reply 'yes, these are my hands' as though there was nothing unusual about this. A part of John had expected the stranger to deny it. He was becoming increasingly more frightened. He stayed firm against the wall while being all too aware that he himself was closest to the window and furthest from the door. He set about to change this. While pressed against the wall he began to make his way towards the debris, building up the courage to ask the most ridiculous question of his life. "Are you... are... ah feck this!" As he made his way along the wall, as if it were a cliff side, the stranger rotated on the spot. As he neared the door, John felt a little more secure. He blurted out his question in a flurry of embarrassment, fear and spit. "Are you an angel?"

The stranger stood there, motionless, until he began to stiffly move his head sideways. He looked at the floor for a moment and then looked at John.

"I do not know," replied the stranger.

"What the fuck kinda answer is that? What do you mean you don't know? If you were an angel you'd flippin' know about it, surely."

In a calm and logical voice the stranger replied, "I do not know what an angel is. Therefore I am unsure as to whether or not I am one."

Dumb founded, John now found himself pressed against the door, and pressing back against him was new found confidence. Once he had said it aloud, John realised how ridiculous his question was. "Tell me, are you on drugs? Drugs is it? You know what, half the street probably heard you break into my home. The last thing I need is the guards around here finding me talking with some druggy. Hole in the roof or not, you gotta get out, lad." The stranger stood there, eyes a little wider, but staring just as intensely. Drip. Drop. Silence.

"Well go on! Get out! Get out!" John had lost nearly all fear of the stranger, massive and powerful he may have been, there was something that carried him without a hint of threat. John lunged his neck and moved his head towards the door. The stranger broke eye contact and looked at the floor. Still with steam rising from his body, he slowly turned his head to look at the door. He stared at the closed door of John's bedroom. Then, like someone awaking from a coma, he turned his head back to once more stare John in the eye.

"What is beyond that boundary?"

"Boundary? Yeah, well, beyond my *door* is what remains of my shitty apartment. And beyond that is a shitty hallway with a shitty staircase. Follow it out the shitty front *boundary* and make your way onto the shitty streets of this shitty city. All right?"

"Why is everything '*shit-ty*'?"

John squinted and slightly turned his head in response to the question.

"What is your deal, buddy? You have to be on something. Look just follow those directions and you'll be on your way."

Drip. Drop. All things considered, John was calmer than most. It was, after all, half four in the morning, in just a few hours it would be Monday work morning. There was a hole in, well, the building. John's chest of drawers was more sawdust than solid and his bed now looked like a bobsled waiting to be released. And to top it all off there was a steaming, naked, angel-come-drug dealer trying to squat in his home. However, the fact that this stranger wasn't taking his leave was really pushing John's patience to its end. Drip. Drop.

"Okay, well right. This has been fun and all but, ah, like I said. I think it's time for you to be on your way. So I'd like you to leave now. Please. Just go."

"But, where am I to go?"

"I don't know, buddy, you know what they say..." he looked at the stranger who was blankly staring back.

"Well maybe *you* don't. But what they say is 'you don't have to go home, but you can't stay here' so you know... the world is your oyster, ah, I set you free, ah, Jesus get the fuck out, I don't know! Just fucking leave."

"For how long?" The shock of the question was clear on John's face.

"Forever, lad. Forever and ever and ever. And if you do decide to drop by some day, try not to do it in the literal sense, okay?"

"But I have nowhere to go. I don't even know where I am."

"I told ya, you're in shitty Cork city. And I have a hole to fix and work to sleep for so..."

John went to lead the stranger out of his room and out of his life. To do so, he started to turn him towards the door by putting his hand on his shoulder.

"Oh, holy shit!" John pulled his hand off of the stranger's back as soon as he touched it. It was like resting his hand on a cooling stove.

"Jesus Christ, just, ah, just follow me and... try not touch anything on the way, okay?"

John let go of his hand and opened the door to the sitting room and walked towards the front door. If you were asked to enter John's apartment and identify the room that had suffered the crash landing, you would be hard pushed to decide between the bedroom and the rest of his home. As John walked through the sitting room, the stranger stayed stationary back in what is best described as the sleeping quarters. John motioned for him to follow. Finally the stranger began to budge and followed John. He stood with an open and cold front door, which led to an even colder hallway. He ushered the way-ward traveler into the hall and out of his life.

"Well, look, you ah, you seem to be fine, and to be honest man, you're not my fucking problem and I, ah..."

John shrugged his shoulders and pushed out the door, making the mistake of making eye contact just as it closed. Turning around, John fell back against the door, hands running through his thinning hair. Exhaling into forearms he listened. Nothing. Not a creak of wood, not a tap of footwork. No evidence of momentum. He waited in silence a moment longer before turning around quickly and grabbing the door handle. An open doorway was filled with a stationary stranger.

"Ah man come on like! What are you doin' standing there? Look, go down the hall and down those steps until you come to the front door. Then pull the blue handle on the wall and get out onto the street, okay?" spoke John as he leaned out of the doorframe with his arm pointing down the hall. He pointed so strongly that his index finger was about to escape his hand. The stranger's gaze followed the outstretched arm and continued down the hall. John watched as he lumbered towards the staircase. John wondered if he was going to be able to use the steps in the dark. Unfortunately, this nugget of thought came too late and John watched as the silhouetted stranger outstretched a leg, missed the first step and careered down the flight of stairs to the first landing. The sound settled. John waited anxiously for one moment before hearing the riggers of twilight banister searching accompanied by the cautious decent onto the next step. Then another, then another.

As the stranger developed his new skill, John murmured beneath his breath; "He fell from the sky, the staircase is nothing."

Perhaps it was denial, perhaps it was the delirium of the a.m. Call it what you will, but John did his best to ignore the realities of the situation at hand and made his way back to the bedroom. In the spirit of ignoring your problems he did the only thing possible upon returning to his room and turned his head straight for the floor. The gaping hole was still there, but if he couldn't see it, well, somehow it was less of a problem. In avoiding a problem he created a conundrum. Instead of seeing the hole above, he was forced to view the impact crater etched in the floorboards. It wasn't the split lumber that concerned him, it was the torched timber. The circle where the stranger had lain was black, with charred veins of split wood emanating from the centre.

Denial is more powerful than belief.

As John lay in the sloping bed, he pulled his bedside locker right against the mattress. This had the dual purpose of resting his head and preventing him from rolling out of the bed and onto the floor. All the while the orange light had snuck quietly back onto the wall. The last time he admired its glow he was without a skylight and without an angel. Turning onto his other side and into the foetal position, John realised it would not be long before he slinked out onto the floor like a snail. Frustrated, he spun around to his original position and slammed, face first into the locker. It recoiled in unison and flipped over once more. Cursing in shades of vocabularies, John stood to place the locker upright. Then, outside the window and towards the street lamp he saw it. All the comforting street lamps in the city cannot prevent the stress that accompanies a naked man with wings on his back slowly waving up at you and the hole in your building. Forehead pressed against the glass, he could still see the stranger through the condensation of his breath. In fact, the degree of slumping was so much that he was closer to jumping out the window than he was to looking through it.

"Go on, Lord, do it. Break the glass and let me fall out the window," spoke John as he desperately looked down at the man below. "The only deal is that the fall has got to kill me, right?"

Just as he was about to climb back into bed the stranger started to shout up at the window.

"What now? I am on the street. Where do I go now?"

A pause and then the rhetoric began, like a broken record the stranger was calling out to John. And just as the flick of a switch turned the dark window of the neighboring apartment from black to yellow, the light bulb of realisation came on in John's head.

That light was from the otherwise desolate home of Mrs O'Flaherty. John would have preferred a helicopter with the letters BBC written across it, at least that way less people would hear about what was happening. Upon seeing the naked gentleman in the alley, Mrs O'Flaherty would undoubtedly call John's landlord. Seeing as John had yet to pay this month's rent, the last thing he needed was to hammer out asteroid repair costs. He opened the window and shouted in the whisper of the desperate.

"Sssh! Sssshhh! Shut up, shut up! Just, shut up." The stranger quietened down. But it was too late.

The outside light belonging to Mrs O'Flaherty was on. Old and feeble she may have been, but she was a strong and determined woman. It was only a matter of moments before she would be at the door. John ran out of his apartment and jumped down the staircase. He flung open the front door and called the stranger inside. Frustration.

"But you directed me onto the shit-ty street. Why now are you calling me back inside?"

"What are you, some kind of comedian, just get the fuck back in!"

He stood there motionless. Motionless and still very, very naked. John ran outside and grabbed him by the back. This time the stranger's skin had cooled somewhat but it was still roasting to the touch. But John was able to direct him back towards the door. As they walked, the stranger stood directly atop a glass bottle and crunched it into sand beneath his foot. John maneuvered them both inside just as Mrs O'Flaherty came on the scene.

Luckily, past instances of ally altercations along with knowledge on the habits of Mrs O'Flaherty gave John the presence of mind to turn off the lights before leaving. With any luck, it would put her off the trail and prevent an unwelcome landlord-tenant conversation. Standing like a burglar in his own home John stood in his bedroom looking out the window until the lights across the way went out. He drew the curtains and pulled the door closed behind him, grabbing trousers en route. In the light of the sitting room the stranger stood once more. John threw the pants toward him and motioned the actions until the stranger was a little more decent. Just then he remembered directing the stranger directly over the glass. "Ah man, sorry about the glass bottle outside, lad. I just, I just didn't want Mrs O'Flavs to see and, ah still. Here, let me see your foot."

He was about to ask him to sit, but the learning curve of the past hour made John drop that idea. Down on one knee, John lifted the stranger's leg to reveal his foot. Nothing. It was not even dirty and there were no cuts. He must have been confused and had selected the wrong leg. He placed it down in order to examine the other foot. Nothing. Not a cut, not a scratch on that one either.

He saw him stand on it, he witnessed the shards, he heard the shatter. But the stranger's foot was flawless. Then John realised that which he had over looked. This stranger, standing before him in the glow of electric light, was completely unharmed. Considering the fact that he burst through tiles and timber, ceilings and floor, he was without harm, without blemish. As John stood upright, he spun around the stranger like a panoramic camera. There were no cuts, no wounds. Nowhere could he even identify a single scratch. Not a hair out of place.

Not one hair. Not one feather.

CHAPTER II

NUMBERS

There is only one type of man, for all men are ordinary. But there are stories, there are myths and there is hope for all that comes built from the ashes of extraordinary moments. It is in these moments of time that ordinary men become immortal.

***

The realization that the stranger had a distinct lack of injuries conjured up questions. Questions that would bare answers. Answers that John was not prepared for.

"I'm sorry, man, what with the whole crash landing I, I didn't even ask. Are you okay?"

The concept did not register.

"I mean are you hurt, are you injured or anything, like? Are you even sore?"

"Sore?" Came the slowly repeated reply from the stranger. "What is the meaning of 'sore'?"

"Yeah, sore. It means in pain. Just, you had one hell of a fall. And you don't even have a bruise. Are you okay?"

"Yes. I am o-k." John stood staring at him. The stare soon became a squint as John's brain began to race. Three fingers grasped a cooling wrist as John rose out the arm of the stranger. He looked at his forearm as he placed his fingers upon him.

"Tell me if this hurts."

He pinched the stranger's forearm.

"Yes, I can feel that."

"No, not can you *feel* it, I want to know does it *hurt* when you feel it, okay?"

He continued to pinch, this time harder. There was no reaction. John pinched and twisted the skin.

"What about that, is that sore, does it hurt or is it uncomfortable?" The stranger took a breath as if he was about to disappoint John, but disappoint, he would not.

"No. I can feel it. But I have no quarrel with it."

By now the skin on the strangers arm was being stretched to its limits. All the while John took note of the fact that the appearance stayed the same. He began to progress further with his experiment. After half explaining and reassuring the stranger of his intentions, John began to lightly slap the forearm. Heavier and heavier slaps became punches. Before long, John was punching the flesh of this stranger with no reaction at all. As a matter of fact, if anything the stranger showed his first signs of amusement. Panting, a pivot placed John before the cutlery drawer. He sighed as he turned to the stranger, steak knife in hand.

"Now again, don't worry. I'm not trying to harm you. I just, well, I just kinda have to see this. You stop me if you feel pain, okay? I mean it, lad, just tell me all right?"

He took the expected silence as the green light. He turned over the palm of his lab rat and began to attempt to prick his finger. Nothing. Nothing from the thumb to the baby and all three fingers in between. By now, John was trying his best to draw blood. It was time for something more drastic.

The gulp in John's throat reflected his actions; the edge of the blade was now pressed against the strangers palm and John looked him in the eyes as he wrapped his fingers around to form a fist. Now the stranger was tightly holding the sharp side of the knife. One more gulp. John pulled the knife out of the closed fist as fast as he could. Where one would expect to feel the thrashing of flesh, the blade simply glided across his skin. There was no blood, only amazement. For in place of blood, John witnessed fine, golden flakes that faded to shimmering dust as they sparkled below the yellow light, before disappearing before his eyes. John looked at the knife, the serrations had been worn clean off and the blade was now smooth, blunt and almost worn through.

It was all John needed. It was all he needed to believe the wings were real, the very same wings that he was still in denial about. John backed away slowly until his back touched the wall. He then slid downwards and slumped into a ball on the floor, desperately trying to process what was happening to him.

"Are you, are you an angel, like?"

"If you will recall, I have already informed you that I do not know what..."

"Ah! Ah! No, no don't pull that one again. Either you are an angel or you're not. Trust me, it's kinda the sort of thing you know." For once, John was not looking at the stranger; he stared straight ahead as he sat. Arms around legs and legs against chest, curled into the tightest ball he could form.

"I do not know that I am an angel, therefore, if it is something I would know, I guess that I am not. No, I am not an angel."

"Jesus Christ, I'm being visited by the angel of grammar! Okay, okay, so if you're not one, then how can you explain those wings coming out of your back, huh?"

The angel of grammar looked over his shoulder and slightly flexed one of his wings before replying, "Do you not have wings?"

"No I do not have flipping wings! So you admit it, they are wings! They are real! Well if you're not an angel, despite clearly having wings, how do you explain the Midas touch with the knife? Or the fact that you came through my roof from a cloud? Huh, where did you come from, don't you remember anything, like?"

The response to the last question instantly calmed John down, for it evoked a change in the stranger. For the first time, he displayed real emotion and it was one of sadness. Not extreme sadness, fleeting it may have been, but it lived long enough that John saw it pass in his face.

"I am afraid that I do not know. I did not expect that there was somewhere to come from. Nor did I realise there was more to remember. I, I must apologise, but I cannot answer your question."

Empathy is like lightning; it can strike out of the blue and in a flash it can leave you devastated.

"I'm sorry, lad, I wasn't trying to upset you, it's just a lot to handle. Do you even know your name?"

Flash.

"Do you even *have* a name?"

Clearly, it strikes the same spot as frequently as it wishes. Unexpectedly, the stranger smiled at John.

"No. I do not have a name; I didn't know one was needed. Do you have a name?"

"John. My name is John Doherty." John held out his arm in an attempt at a handshake. The stranger looked down at John's hand, looked John in the face, smiled and said, "That is your hand, John."

John spoke slowly "yes, you got me there. I'm trying to shake your hand."

"Why ever would you do that?"

John's arm stayed outstretched, albeit slightly limp as he replied "Because, it's what you do when you introduce yourself to somebody."

Extended hands met to shake for the first time, John couldn't help but notice that the stranger's skin was still incredibly hot. The encounter waned as John couldn't but help look past his face, over his shoulders and stare intently at the plume of white feathers that were rising above the shoulders of the hand he was shaking. At long last, it was time for the inspection.

John rounded the stranger and began to fully accept what was stood in his home. This was real. This was happening. There was an angel before him. From his shoulder blades grew stalks of tremendous diameter, they carried the wings of an albatross, perhaps larger. They were flawlessly adorned with talc white feathers. As John rotated on point the feathers seemed to glisten in the light, as though diamonds were threaded and intertwined into every weave of this magical fabric. Not a single feather was missing, not one ruffled, none were out of place.

"Amazing. Can, like, are you able to move them? Like, can you open them or do they ju—"

With that, the stranger's shoulders rose and his body lurched as he spread his wings. Without even being fully expanded, the wings already were a few metres in width. They swooped open in an arc, before powerfully snapping into place, the left wing split the coffee table into shards as the right wing sheared clean through a worn armchair.

"Jesus Christ! Be careful with those things!"

John jumped, arms outstretched, against the strangers back, desperately trying to force the wings to retract. The stranger looked over his shoulder at John's fleeting arms, which were shaking with pressure and began to contract his wings. They folded up neatly behind his back. Breathless, John was drawn to where the wings fused to blades. In particular, he examined the follicle where the first of the feathers grew. Slowly, he pinched one single feather between his fingers and pulled, ever so softly.

The stranger recoiled instantly, spinning away from John and leaping backwards to the other side of the room. The two men stared at each other once more, John looking apologetic, the stranger with wide, worried eyes.

"I'm sorry! I'm sorry. I didn't mean to... I just, I just wanted to see if they came off. You know, like with birds."

The two men stared clean through the silence that filled the gulf between them. John's apology was enough to cross the divide.

"I'm sorry, I won't do it again."

John couldn't tell if it hurt the stranger or if it just made him uncomfortable. Either which way, he knew the kitchen knife was going nowhere near those wings.

Once the stranger was calmed and reassured, the adrenaline of the early morning had worn off and John was exhausted. By now it was bright outside and the day was soon to be starting. John made his way to the closet and pulled a spare blanket from the shelves.

"Here you go. With the heat coming off ya, I don't think you'll freeze or anything, but this is just in case. You can sleep on the sofa, since you haven't broken that yet. I don't know what's going on here, but it can wait until tomorrow, it'll have to. I have work in the morning, after that, we can sort the roof out first and then what to do with you after. We'll get you a name too."

John walked into the doorway of his room and stood with his back to the stranger who stood silent, blanket in hand.

"It's too late in the night to be naming angels."

He swung the door closed behind him and sighed. At that moment his alarm went off and so too did the street lamp.

***

The first few are priceless. It varies from time to time. Depending on the gravity of the situation. But the first few seconds after you wake truly are priceless, because you are unaware of what kind of day you have awoken to. They are the moments spent hurtling towards reality, before the inevitable impact of realisation takes hold. No matter what grievance, despite the manner of hardship or day ahead, you have escape in those first few seconds. But despite being priceless, these seconds do not come without a cost and the bursar *never* leaves without his pay.

Having hit the snooze button, John made a break for escape in the form of sleep, it was only half an hour that he would get but it would have to do. The alarm waits for no one, especially the poor. And in those first few seconds of wide eyelids, John was free. Until reality came drip dropping down the hole in his ceiling. The room was freezing. The smell of the neglected apartment above filled John's lungs. The damp of the Irish climate had taken its toll. He found the cleanest looking clothes among the debris and got dressed. Upon opening the door John was greeted by the stranger standing in the exact same repose as when he left the room, he stood still clutching the blanket. It was the first time in a very long time that John hand been greeted by a smile from the first person of the day. Usually he was battling influenza and bad manners on the number 5 bus.

John was disappointed that the stranger was still there. A part of him expected that he would have fled in the night. In fact he didn't care if he evaporated since he saw him last. However, the smile was almost worth the reality. 'Click', and the bread would soon become toast. John stood there rubbing his eyes, as if hoping a genie would appear, he was beyond exhaustion. The stranger was simply smiling.

"What is that smell, John?"

"Breakfast. Sometimes lunch and dinner too. I have to go to work."

John spread butter across the black of his toast while thinking of what was best to do. He couldn't handle bringing the stranger outside, but he really was in no position to stay home from work. Click, John was making toast for his guest.

"Here you go, eat that and then sit down and, just get some sleep or something. Do NOT under any circumstances turn anything on or off. Oh and don't even THINK of opening the door to anyone. And don't even think of walking out that front door. Do you hear me? Mrs O'Flavs didn't catch us but that doesn't mean she's not onto us."

The stranger simply stood there smiling. John couldn't tell from his expression if he had just been overloaded with commands or if he just didn't understand a single one of them.

"Right, okay so you're clear on what not to do, correct?" said John as he nodded his head.

The stranger nodded back.

"Well all right then, I'll see you in few hours. Remember, don't fuck anything up okay?" and as he fixed in place a bag on his shoulders, curtains parted for prying eyes as John walked out of the alley and across the bridge to town where he climbed aboard the number 5.

Working in the lumberyard of a construction whole-sellers was a cold job, but this cold job would provide a warm night for John. He would stay a little after work and 'borrow' a few pieces of stock to repair what he could, at least for the moment.

John had worked through days where he was sure he had left the front door open. Those were distracting days. John had worked though days where he was certain the stove was burning his building to the ground. Those were distracting days. But never had he imagined how distracting it would be to have left an un-attended heavenly body with the mind of a Labrador alone in his home. Today brought 'distracting' to a whole new level. As he laboured he was consumed with visions of Mrs O'Flavs talking to the authorities as guardaí dragged the stranger off in a wagon.

For the entire day, he was a man stranded on the island of his thoughts. Was this stranger really an angel? How could he be? Angels are all knowing beings that come down to tell you to change your ways and to stop gambling so much, to live the life of virtue or face the red man himself. They were heavenly pregnancy tests for the virgin elite. They came with either good news or news of the apocalypse. They came with grace and golden light with clouds at their feet. But this guy? This guy probably doesn't even know what feet are. News of the apocalypse? This guy doesn't even know his own name.

The other men of the yard did not notice that John was a million miles away from their banter talk about women and stories of things that never happened. Even if they did notice, it was not in the remit of an Irish man to genuinely ask was another feeling okay. Equally, it certainly wasn't expected for a man to reply to such an un-asked question with his true feelings. The men worked away, as did John.

All the rationalising that an idle mind can muster could not compete with what John had seen for himself. If this stranger was not an angel, then how could John explain the gold and the knife, the crash landing and lack of injury, the boiling flesh and wondrous wings? No, when John got home, he was going to need answers.

After telling the usual late evening stragglers that he was waiting for a lift, John told Tony, the yard manager that he'd volunteer for the lock up tonight. As he waited impatiently for the last of the men to pack up, Tony shouted across the yard,

"Hey, John, don't forget the pad lock on the side gates when you leave, all right?"

When the last of the men left, John wasted no time in filling his backpack with the few slates that he could carry. He also took a wooden pallet in which he jammed miscellaneous boards into the gap between bottom and top. With the universal blue rope that signified a degenerate up to no good, John dragged the pallet to the gates, slapped on the lock, pushed a spry vertebrae back into place and made way for the bus stop. Down the street he looked like a man who was after suffering some manner of psychotic break, one who now believed himself to be a husky, pulling a passenger-less sled.

"Ha, you've got to be kidding me, boy! Not a *hope* am I letting you onto my bus with all that stuff! Try the next one or get a taxi, boy!" The sound of compressed air closing the doors was a song that John was to hear replayed several times that night.

"No, no, no. Section four, paragraph seven of the bus drivers' directive clearly states that no offensive items may be allowed onto any city bus."

"Offensive items? It's a pile of timber jammed into a palate of more timber! Ah come on, lad, I'm no threat to anyone!"

The bus driver closed his eyes and leaned forward towards the door, stomach spilling over the wheel as he spoke.

"Section four, paragraph seven of the bus drivers' directive clearly sta—"

"Ah, forget it, I'll get the next one! You want an offensive item? Well fuck you and your precious fucking bus." From an outside point of view, it wasn't John's highest point to date. But neither was it his lowest.

Finally, after five buses and two rain showers, a bus slowly rolled up to the stop. In fact, it rolled a litter further beyond it. John was less than optimistic. But that was before he saw the peanut of a man behind the wheel with spectacles like shot glasses. His hair had grown so far out of his ears that it had begun to droop. He couldn't have been sure, but by first inspection John assumed the driver to be about a hundred and twelve years old and completely blind. Wide eyes and cautious, John climbed onto the bus. He lugged the mass of wood along beside him as slates clambered in his bag. John held out the hand that had been holding his fare for the past few hours. He was met with a limp handshake and the bus began to roll down the road once again. John counted his blessings and lugged his cargo away from the door.

By the time John was in the familiar surrounds of the alley it was some time near ten p.m. The immediate hallway was as far as the lumber was coming that night, rain or no rain. Even more exhausted than when he left, John found the energy to quickly scale the staircase, he was anxious about what he would find upstairs. As the key tumbled in the lock, John could hear the murmuring of low voices. The door creaked open to reveal darkness. "Hello?" spoke John as he flicked on the lights.

"Hello, John. Did you have a prosperous day at work?" Had that been anyone else, they would have been met with a reply riddled in sarcasm. But the question came with such sincerity that John just stood there. Furthermore, it was said with a smile, being greeted with a smile when he came home was unprecedented. In fact, simply being greeted by someone in his home after work was precedent in itself. All of a sudden, the weight of the slates and the weight of the day were lifted from his shoulders, in that one simple moment of sincerity.

"How was the weather today, was it cold and partly blustery, John? And, I was thinking that maybe we could go into town and see the street food fair next week, it seems to be full of activities from what I hear."

The stranger's comments were almost more shocking than his initial entrance. Not just the flow of his speech, but the topics of conversation. A few hours ago this guy didn't even know what toast was.

"What are you talking about?"

"The weather, John. I am interested in knowing how you experienced the day. Also, I thought it would be good to 'check out' the food fair."

John's eyes began to squint as he put two and two together. He got four. It made sense now; the sounds of the voices were from the radio, which was on at low volume, and the room was decorated in the style of a newspaper graveyard.

John's flat was consumed with islands and stacks of old newspapers. It wasn't that he loved to read as much as he loved the idea of the newspapers. In many a way, they were an outlet of his loneliness. For every time he would buy a newspaper he would have a quick chat with the person behind the counter in the shop. Often John would buy the same paper twice in one day, just to meet someone else. He also liked the current affairs of the local papers, keeping up with them made him feel less isolated, less alone. There was however, one book that John had received for free in a newspaper a few years previous. He had read it to the point of being able to recite it. It was precious to him and so he kept it under his pillow. Worn and tattered it was one of the few positive constants in his life.

"You've, ah, you've been learning, haven't you?" John smiled as he looked from the papers to the stranger.

"You've been listening to the radio all day and catching up on local events."

"Not just local events, John, those parchments contain global and international news."

John was amused at how concerned the stranger was as he picked up one of the newspapers and pointed to it as he spoke. He flicked through the pages and showed John the stories that interested him the most. Then, with the excitement of a child, he ruffled the pages closed, turned to face John and frantically said; "John, you must explain something to me."

He threw the paper down on the remaining sofa and spun around, nearly knocking John over in the process. The stranger lunged down on all fours and began to comb through the newspapers. The tips of his wings fluttered as he searched and, once he had found what he was looking for, his wings parted slightly before quickly shutting again. The updraft created by the wings lifted the stranger to his feet and spread the remaining newspapers away like a blast radius.

"Here, here it is. I was to wonder, John, in this issue all they seem to be talking about is 'the parade', look see, the whole issue is full of it. But they have not made reference to it on the radio stations. Why is this, John, has 'the parade' been cancelled? I really would enjoy that parade if it were still to occur."

The answer John was about to give would only further add to the oddity of a scenario in which he found himself. Not

47

alone did this stranger not know who or where he was, the stranger did not know *when* he was. It was now April and the stranger had been reading newspapers that had piled up in the sitting room, he had been reading one from back in March. The stranger was looking forward to St Patrick's Day. John began to explain.

"See, these papers are printed daily, and then the information kinda becomes useless, like for events and things. You know how to keep track because they print the date of publication on them, see this one is over a month old."

John pointed to the date: 8th March, 1984.

"And today is April the fifteenth, so you've missed the parade. But ah, don't you worry like, you didn't miss much. Besides, there is one every year."

The stranger looked excited by this concept. As John spoke to him, he pulled a jumper off the back of the couch, despite spending the day becoming a man of this world the stranger was still topless.

"Really? Every year? For how long and why, John?"

The stranger began to forage his way into the garment. John spoke about the parade.

"See, he's the patron saint of Ireland because, well because he got rid of all the snakes out of Ireland and, well, I guess he probably did other things too. I don't really know. People don't really know either, but it's a good excuse to not go to work and drink for the day instead so nobody really questions the whole thing. Mind you, he didn't do a very good job, I still know a good few snakes myself."

The stranger poked his head out of the jumper with a confused look on his face. "You *know* snakes personally, John?" as he continued to try and fit into the jumper.

John rolled his eyes as he spoke, "No, it's, it's a joke is all. I wouldn't expect an angel to get it." John paused at the mention of the word before continuing.

"Actually, that was something I meant to ask you about. I was thinking about it at work. You say you're not an angel and I believe you, sort of. At least, I think you're being honest when you say you really don't know, but I still have my doubts. And with wings like that, can you blame me, like?"

John was smiling as he stared at the stranger who had successfully put his arms through the sleeves, his chest was covered but John had somehow managed to forget about the wings. The jumper looked like some sort of wooly, aran tank-top on the stranger. John attempted to help him.

"Let's see, let's try to pull this down over... no, that's not working. Can you like, can you suck them in or something like?"

The stranger tightened his wings against his back so that they were completely flush with his body.

"That's better, yeah hang on."

John managed to pull the jumper most of the way down his back. The fibres were like those of a harp, some beginning to give already. John rummaged through the kitchen drawers and pulled out the scissors. Tailoring was never a trade of his but, then again, this really was a one off production. He cut slits down the back of the jumper and directed the wings out.

"There, that looks a little more comfortable. Still, not exactly ideal for going out. But yeah, it's things like that that make me wonder, buddy. Like, what exactly do you remember?"

The stranger turned his head sideways and stared as though he was looking through the very floor. John continued.

"Really, try hard to remember. I know we're trying to unravel the meaning of life here and it's probably not the best time, but do you want some spaghetti?"

The stranger did not break his gaze.

"I mean, don't get me wrong, I want to know, but I'm also starving and I'll take a safe bet and say you haven't eaten all day."

As the stranger became more solemn, John waited for a reaction.

"Okay, you just take a moment there and I'll start dinner, don't be expecting anything amazing here, like."

Under the sink were two cabinet doors, neither in line with the other and hinges that were unmatched. John opened one and produced a pot that was so worn, it looked as though an iron caster traded with it. The black of the pot was matched only by the rings of the cooker. The click of the gas and hum of the flame relaxed the atmosphere. Pulling the lids off of spaghetti cans, John was half way through the stranger's first taste of Italy. As John sang below his breath the stranger broke his vow of silence.

"John, I do not wish that you think of me a liar."

Genuine concern carried this comment into John's ears.

"Before, when you asked me what I remember I told you that all I could recall was waking on your floor. Well I have remembered more. I promise that, at the time of your question, I was truthful. Please do not think me a liar."

John walked from the stove and reassured the stranger that he believed him. He did believe him. He encouraged him to continue.

"Well, I have remembered more, it was today while I was reading. I did not tell you when you came in as I worried you would think me a liar. Before I came to be on your floor, I remember falling. I remember falling for a very long time."

John moved closer and sat on the arm of the couch.

"Where were you falling from? Were you scared? Why were you falling?"

"I am sorry, but I do not remember where it was I left behind, or why. But no, John, I was not scared. In fact I was happy. I remember feeling safe and secure. If I am to be honest, I was very surprised when I struck the roof of your home. That is all I remember, perhaps more will return to me."

As he nodded, John walked to stir the spaghetti and he turned the ring off. From the counter he revealed a loaf of bread, which he split, buttered and plated. Over this he tilted the pot and washed with spaghetti. Two pint glasses that were stolen from the bar by the river were half filled with milk.

"Voila. Well, buddy, it's not much, like. But it's ours."

John smiled as he placed the meal on the stranger's lap, the coffee table still lay split in the centre of the room. Upon returning with flower-embroidered cutlery, the smile disappeared from his face. The stranger looked at his plate as though it were crawling with snakes.

"Ah please don't tell me I have to fucking explain this to you too! It's dinner, food like!"

"No, John, I know what it is. But I am afraid I am not hungry. Not at all. I do not think I could eat this."

Relief from dodging a tutorial was replaced by disbelief.

"But, you haven't eaten a bite all day. Plus, you crashed through my ceiling and burned my floor boards with your radioactive skin, you have to be peckish after something like that."

The stranger just smiled apologetically. As John shrugged his shoulders his manners, like his hunger, had gotten the better of him. And with a churning mouth, John continued the search for answers.

"I was also thinking, while I was lugging wood around the yard, do you know himself at all?"

"Do I know '*himself*'?"

"Yeah, do you know him, like, is he real?"

The stranger narrowed his brow as he looked at John.

"Don't look at me like that, you know who I am on about. The big man in the sky, the big Kahoona, the alpha and the omega? God! Do you know him?"

A day spent waiting for answers was stood up by disappointment.

"I know you, John. You are the only person I know. So unless you are 'God' then I do not know him."

John smiled, he may not have been breaking bread with Gabrielle, but at least this guy had a sense of humour. The stranger continued, "I'm sorry to disappoint you, John, but I don't even know who I am, let alone who God is."

"You know what, lad, you're right. We still don't have a name for ya, do we? I was thinking about that at work too today, didn't do much else there really. Well, I was going to give ya a kind of biblical name, but since you wouldn't know mother Teresa if you fell on top of her, we can throw that idea out of the window. Have you any ideas?"

"Yes, I saw some names in the newspapers today and I figured that as everyone appears to have a name, I thought that perhaps I should try to have one also. How about 'Richard' is that a good name?"

The squinting eyes of disapproval rocked inside of John's shaking head.

"Trust me, buddy, you don't want that name. It doesn't lend itself to nice nicknames. Anything else?"

"Yes, I thought that 'Katie' sounded nice. What would you think of Katie as a name for me, it seems to have a good sound to it, does it not?"

"It does, it does. But am, that name is more one that a girl would have, third time lucky perhaps?"

The stranger paused and thought for just a moment.

"Vincent?" John smiled and extended his hand once more.

"Vincent, nice to meet you, I'm John." And with that, John shook the hand of the first friend he had made in quite some time.

Keep your friends close.

***

The hot tap was running, the cold first being flushed out. John had started to do the washing up as the sauce lifted from the base of the pot, John covered Vincent's plate of spaghetti with aluminum foil. In the background, Vincent stood facing the wall with an out stretched hand. Over and over he practiced introducing himself as John washed his plate.

"You know, not everyone is going to have the same reaction to you as me. Before we can decide what it is we're going to do with you, Vincent, we're going to have to cover up those wings. I have an old trench coat in my wardrobe, you might look a little funny in it, but it should keep you a bit more low key than that jumper you're sporting."

"But why do I have hide my wings, John?"

Turning off the tap and drying his hands, John was taken aback by the sheer naïvety of Vincent.

"Because, Vincent, a person is okay, like. A person is rational. But *people*, people are animals. There are so many bad things that could happen to you if everybody knew about you. From the religious nuts who would take advantage of you, to the people who would turn you into a circus attraction. People might even want to harm you, now I doubt that's really possible after everything I've seen over the last twenty-four hours, but you can't afford to take that chance."

Vincent replied in tones of naivety, "John, I am sure that people would have kinder hearts than to do things such as that. I was thinking today that we should go and tell… "

"No! We can't… " John cut across Vincent and turned to face him. He put both his hands on his shoulders as he continued "…not yet and not to anyone. You don't understand enough yet, but there really are people out there who will want to hurt you. People who won't understand how important you are. So don't make any decisions without me, okay? We're in this together."

It worked. Vincent looked deeply confused and frightened. Men all have their ulterior motives and will put their wants of self-gain far above the needs of others. John was no exception.

John so desperately needed Vincent, but he had to do all that was in his power to convince him that it was the other way around.

"But don't worry, it's not all bad, there is probably something great out there for you but, until we figure things out, it's best that you keep those wings of yours under wraps, okay? Remember, from now on it's you and me, buddy, you and me the whole way."

Vincent looked calmed and reassured, and John could see it written all over his face. He found it amusing; that something of such God like powers, such ability and sheer strength could be swayed by such thoughts and moved by such simple words. Although he seemed to be only learning the most basic of realities, John could see how intelligent he was. But as John returned to the sink to dry the ware, and as Vincent resumed introduction practice, John felt an unease settle. It was sudden and consuming, like a balloon of tension had burst above his head and the whole room was blanketed with a foreboding sensation. Maybe it was just the last of adrenaline leaving his system. Perhaps it was a delayed reaction to the reality in which he found himself.

Or maybe, it was the realisation that, irrespective of where tomorrow would go, his life would never be the same. It is so easy to be lulled into the comfort that comes with routine, even if it's not a very good routine. The longer you go through the motions, the more violently you are ripped from the security of the life you have been leading. The routine may not be the most exciting, but it is secure and above all else it is constant. With the loss of routine comes the risk of something new. Something new may be good or it may be the start of something terrible, and here is where the worry lies. John was now out of routine and not knowing where he was going scared him.

He realised that the main risk lay with Vincent. If John was going to make any good of this situation, he would have to safe guard it against Vincent himself. Good intentioned as he was, his life was by no means a success. John realised that Vincent could be a chance to turn things around. As of the crash landing, he had left his old life behind and he was damned if he was going to miss this opportunity. His roof was in pieces and so was his life. It was time to rebuild both.

"Vincent, I want to explain a few things to you." John motioned for them both to sit down together. I have to go to work again tomorrow, but I'll be finished early, around three p.m. After that we can go to town and I can show you around the city."

"The shit-ty city of Cork?"

"Okay, look. Firstly, it's *'shitty'* not 'shit-*ty'* and secondly it's not that shitty. I was pisssed off and stressed when I said that. But yeah, I'll come straight home and then we can have a bit of a walk around the city while it's still bright, see if the world outside my flat jogs your memory."

Then John remembered the more pressing job at hand; the ceiling in his bedroom and the roof of the building. Where would he start? He figured that the best thing to do was to at least bring the supplies up from the front entrance. He asked Vincent for help.

As the two walked through the hall, John found the situation surreal, to say the least. In his head, at least to some degree, an angel was wearing his torn jumper and was about to help him lift stolen roof tiles and lumber up to his apartment. And if he wasn't an angel, then what was he? One thing at a time. When he tried to lift the bag of slates, John questioned how he got them home in the first place. By now, the exhaustion had taken the better of him.

"Vince, could you maybe help with the..." pointing to the bag on the floor. With that, Vincent picked up the bag as if it were empty, the muscles in his arms barley flexing beneath the jumper. He slung the bag over his shoulders and put one massive hand across an end board of the pallet. He lifted it clean off of the floor, like a crane lifting a cardboard box, he could have stood there all night and not once broken a sweat. Effortlessly, he carried the supplies back to the apartment. Luckily, as well as above, no one lived below John, it was not a desirable building, but what it lacked in character it made up for in sheer loneliness.

Back in the sitting room, John directed Vincent to put the stuff down until they had assessed the damage.

"Why have we brought these items into your home, John?"

"Because, that little stunt of yours left this home a little worse for wear. Just give me a few minutes to..."

John had walked into his bedroom in order to assess where to start. He was speechless. The hole was gone. The entire ceiling had been repaired, the floor too had been replaced where Vincent had landed. Even the leg of the bed had been mended. All that remained were the veins of split and burned wood that stretched beneath the bed.

John creaked the floorboards as he turned on the spot to see Vincent standing in the sitting room.

"Did you... Vincent how... how do you... what happened here?"

Vincent simply stood there, smiling at John. He was amazed, he was relieved, but then came the sweeping terror of realisation; if Vincent really mended all of the damage, then where did he get the supplies? More worrying still, if anyone saw him, did they follow him home?

CHAPTER III

REVELATIONS

Human nature is one of the many unusual characteristics that separate man from the other animals. But there is instinct in your emotion, despite the drive for basic needs such as sleep, food and warmth, there are emotions that force a man to forget such things. Some can drive a man wild, others, mad. One such of these is your ability to conjure denial in order to survive reality. It is a mechanism built so deep in your psyche that it contradicts the logical brain. Denial can save a man just as it can destroy one.

Never under estimate its powers or its limitations.

***

For it was denial that allowed John to turn away from a smiling angel without asking a single question as to the series of events which led to the repair of his home. In time, he would have to know, the other side of human nature would see to that. But for now, John had a sleep debt to pay and he was well over due. As he stripped down to his underwear he was once more filled with a brief ominous feeling as his trousers slid past his ankles and lay atop the veins of scorched timber. The weight of denial.

After those closed-lid hours that felt like seconds, John arose from bed like an action replay, pulling his trousers back on and breaking scene to rummage for a 'clean' t-shirt. Creaking floors led him back to the sitting room. Again he was welcomed by a morning smile, this time it had a name attached.

"Heya, Vincent. How did you sleep, buddy?"

Walking into the cove that was his kitchen, he noticed that the blanket he had given Vincent two nights previous, was neatly folded on the couch of the windowless sitting room.

"You did sleep didn't you? Vince? Like, I mean you *do* sleep, right?"

"I was listening to the radio. It was the same show that I listened to in the day time hours. I enjoyed it because I knew what they were going to say."

John shook his head and filled the kettle. "I'll take that one as a no then. I'm having a boiled egg, am I putting one on for you?"

Vincent informed John that he still was not hungry, and not to worry.

John lit the gas ring of the stove and placed a pan of water containing a single egg over it. He walked back towards his bedroom and asked Vincent to call him when the water started to boil. As the pan began to vibrate atop the stove, Vincent stood diligently beside it.

The dancing orange of the flame marred the brilliant blue of his eyes. He was both doing his duty for John and fascinated by the force of nature that is so often taken for granted. He leaned in closer to inspect, so close that the flame literally caressed his very eyes, the flame now curving around the smooth of his eyes. A mere mortal would have long since singed the lashes from their lids. But Vincent, naive of his abilities, simply enjoyed the beauty that was hidden in surroundings consumed by ugliness. He looked up to see John walk back into the room with a rather large coat in hand.

"Right, well, like I said, this coat isn't much but it'll hide those wings of yours for the mean time. I'll leave it here, it'll be a little project for you while I'm at work, try it on and see what way they best fit in, yeah? Jesus, Vincent, that pan is nearly fucking empty, take it off the boil there while there's still water in it!"

John was about to yell words of caution before remembering the circumstances in which he was now living. Instead he watched as Vincent grabbed the metal pot on either side with both hands. The metal would have scalded the skin of any man but Vincent did so without so much as a quiver. John once more explained to him that he was on a half day at work. After explaining the length of a day, the concept of a half-day and finally the workings of a half-day from work it was time to leave.

"Right, that clock reads 'half past eight' and when it changes to three o'clock I'll be home, okay? Remember, when I get home we'll go into town and, well, I don't know, I've never taken an angel to town before. Ah, I guess, I guess we'll get chips. Or at least you can watch me get chips."

John cracked a smile as he walked out of the apartment. As per usual, swaying curtains and prying eyes guided him down the alley. From the moment he hit the street his mind was once more racing. All day at work he was an island, you can't exactly ask your co-workers how to best handle a god like creature who, at the moment, was using your apartment as a catwalk for wing concealment. As far as John was concerned, he had a real life angel at his disposal and John was going to benefit from him. He just didn't know how yet.

As he laboured in the yard he of course succumbed to the thoughts of temptation. It was only human. He thought of every possible manner of exploitation imaginable. The media alone would set him up for life. What about the Americans? They would eat this guy up, live shows in Las Vegas at night every night. Or maybe he could cut out the middleman, sell him straight to the Vatican. Actually, he spent quite a while thinking about that one. How exactly do you go about selling an angel to the pope? His wandering mind did not rest for water there. He thought about harvesting Vincent's strength directly. With his God-like powers, John could have anything he wanted. But, in truth, these thoughts lay at the back of John's mind. He couldn't help thinking this way, they were the flashes of thought that you experience simply by being human and wanting more. Contemplating what may be, what you may have, irrespective of how you get it. These nether reaches of the brain belong in the jungle of the mind. For despite all the temptation that came with what he had been handed in the night, there came the over shadowing of what John had *actually* been handed in the night. And that was a decent person. This was something that John had not experienced directly in a long time.

There was something innocent about Vincent, something genuine in his make up that kept the thoughts of corruption at bay. But most of all, John felt that the responsibility of this way-ward traveler fell on his shoulders. John personally knew the sting that was the signature of neglect. It is a pain that never leaves you. Besides, if this guy really was an angel then angels must be real. That meant that God might be real. John thought of the trouble he would be in for forcing an angel to rob the post office and that alone just wasn't worth it.

Back from work at a reasonable hour, John marched along Barrack Street and turned off onto the dead-ending alley of his building. Behind him he heard the creaking door and a voice that creaked even louder. Her words sent his face plunging into his hands.

"I know."

It was the voice of Mrs O'Flaherty. She stood in the doorway of her own building before she began to crawl out. In fact, she shared more of a likeness with a tortoise than she did anything else. Her humped back loomed like a shell high above her shoulders. Her head was supported by rolls of skin that would conjure images of some sort of wax turkey model that had been left in the sun for too long. Of course, John could never be certain of her actual age but he was sure she lay somewhere between eighty and eight hundred. In fact, she was probably closer to the big man upstairs than Vincent was.

"I know," repeated the elderly woman.

John turned to see a reiterating Mrs O'Flaherty now standing in the middle of the thin alley.

"Good evening Mrs O'Flavs. I'd love to stay and talk but I'm just coming in the door fro—"

"It's O'*Flaherty* you pup! And I know about him." She narrowed her eyes, you could almost taste the delight she experienced from sticking her nose in his business. She was finding the situation so delicious that if she had any more information she'd be gaining calories.

"Look, Mrs O'*Flaherty*," John grinned, "like I was saying, I'm really tired. Now, I don't know what you *think* you might have heard but I can assure you, you're probably just confused."

"Don't talk to me like that you little shite! I know what I saw, and I saw him-flying around at night, mending that roof of yours."

John was dead in the water. Nothing, nothing was the best thing he could say. He locked eyes with Mrs O'Flaherty and it was deafening. There, in the glint of her eyes, lay the answers to all the questions he was going to ask. Most importantly, he saw satisfaction. It was the satisfaction of catching John out. As if that revelation wasn't enough, she continued;

"That's right, not such a smart mouthed little bollocks now, are ya? I heard all the commotion two nights ago. But it wasn't until last night that I actually saw him with my own two eyes. I saw you were late home last night from where ever the hell it is you go, and then I heard the clambering on the roof. I seen him swoop in and out and in and out of that hole in the roof like finch from a birdhouse. In and out he flew with timbers and tiles. Oh yes, I seen him. And I'm going straight to our holy father, Father Declan. And then, after I pray for your sinful soul, I'm going to the papers."

The alley began to fill as concentrated glee spewed from Mrs O'Flaherty. John's sails were still shot, it was time to sink or swim. He knew she was telling the truth. Evidently she knew a little more than John himself. He peered straight into her eyes and instantly knew that there was to be no halfway house on the matter. The only thing left to do was lie.

"Ah, Mrs O'Flavs! Where do you come up with these stories! You're a treasure of the city you are, storyteller extraordinaire! Commotion the other night? You know well that I'm in bed for ten and sleep straight through the night. That's some imagination you have on you!"

If his plan had worked as well as it had pissed her off, he would have been boiling the kettle by now.

"Just because I'm old doesn't mean I'm stupid. I *know* you're harbouring him up there!"

"Harbouring who? I'm no kidnapper if that's what you're saying!"

"An *angel*. You're harbouring an angel."

It is amazing, even though you may be dancing around a problem, trying your best to diffuse it, but all it takes is for someone to call it out into the day. Once you hear it aloud it can send your heart crashing into the pit of your stomach. Speaking about something out loud makes it real. There is no taking it back once it is out. Many a problem has been lived through by virtue of the fact that no one ever spoke of it.

The cracks began to show as the not so silver tongue of John began to dry at the glands.

"Okay, I was joking with you until now, Mrs O'Flavs, but I really don't know what you're on about. I promise. In the name of our holy father above, I swear on the baby Jesus that there is no harbouring of angels, least not in this part of the city."

Having been in a church fewer times than a vampire, John stood there with his left hand over his chest like some confused patriot. His promises were fake, but the beads of sweat were real. Her eyes narrowed.

"On the baby Jesus? Fine then, I believe you."

A sigh of relief was pleading to be released. Mrs O'Flaherty continued, "If your apartment isn't a camp for sacred angels then you won't mind me coming up for a cup of tea then, will you?"

The sigh of relief was swallowed right down to the pit of his gut.

"Just coming up the stairs, the two of us! John and his good old neighbour MRS O'FLAHERTY." John did not know why he was even bothering to shout, Vincent could barely follow direct instructions, let alone pick up on nuances shouted through the walls. In fact Vincent was probably up there practicing his introduction to Mrs O'Flaherty. But still, John could not let her see him. She had threatened to call his landlord and alert Father Declan straight away if he didn't allow her up for a 'cup of tea'. John continued to tell her she was confused, but he had no other choice. He clawed at his last hope.

"Yep, just opening the door, the two of us, ALONE."

"Ah shut the feck up and open the door, ya little shite, ya."

As she barged past the threshold John was already devising an explanation. But as it transpired, Vincent had taken more of the hint than John had given him credit for. As Mrs O'Flavs stood in the kitchen, Vincent was nowhere to be seen. She disappointedly scurried around the apartment. John looked at his bedroom, the door was closed. Knowing that there was no key in the bedroom door, he could only hope that Vincent would have the knowhow to keep the door shut. Returning from the shoulder-width sliver that was John's bathroom, she stood in the centre of the apartment. She looked at his bedroom door, then to John and back to the door once more.

She wasn't taking excuses of dirty underwear as any form of deterrent. She pressed down on the handle of his bedroom door. John's hope was hopeless.

The door swung open and Mrs O'Flaherty gasped. John walked in from the main doorway and collapsed on the kitchen counter. What would he do now? What could he do now? Mrs O'Flaherty would never share Vincent. John was devastated.

"I don't believe it. You've hidden him, you've hidden him away somewhere you unholy little shit!"

John sprang from the counter and raced into his bedroom. He stood there with his neighbour and his neighbour alone. No Vincent, no angel cowering in the corner. Just the cracks of black timber that whispered he had once been.

"What have you done with him? Ha? Where are ya hiding him?"

John tried his best to hide a cacophony of emotions that ranged from relief to despair. As John slowly looked around the bedroom and strained backwards to peer under the bed, he told Mrs O'Flaherty that it was just the two of them in the apartment.

"Yep, just the two of us! So how about that cup of tea?"

"I'd sooner drink a cup of me own piss than the poison you's splash down my throat. I seen him and I'll see him again. And when I do..."

Narrowed eyes and pointed fingers took chorus over her fading threats as she hobbled out of the apartment. If blessings can come in disguise than this was a blight in a blanket.

"You can come out now, Vincent. Vincent?
Vincent?"

But he was not hiding. Vincent had gone.

***

Vincent tuned the radio from station to station as he looked up at the clock. Nine forty-five. John had been gone less than two hours, Vincent had tuned into every station at least once and he couldn't find anything new to read in the apartment. Despite being all powerful, it seemed Vincent was all fed up. As the radio hummed in the background, Vincent walked into John's bedroom. Moving as though he were in a museum, Vincent tilted his head backwards to look at the ceiling. He stood there, blankly staring at where the hole had been. Eyes forward he walked towards the window. Pressing his head against the glass, he peered down the alley to where the street met the world. On this plain, no one can resist temptation.

At least Vincent remembered to don the trench coat that John had pulled out for him. Beneath, he still wore the jumper from the night before. Vincent was ready for town.

Emerging to the street, he enjoyed a rarity in Ireland; sunlight. But like all things that are rare, it was glorious and as the light bathed down atop his face, Vincent closed his eyes and tilted his head upwards. Above him the ceiling was gone, instead there was just the endless sky, which was another thing he had left a hole in.

As cars jostled past and busses waited for breath at traffic lights, Vincent was overcome with the sites that lay before him. He walked straight onto the road without care for the traffic light that had just turned green at the corner to his right. The number 17 came to a screeching halt just feet before him. The driver shouted and cursed as Vincent stood in the middle of the road, oblivious to how close he was to either blowing his cover or else being blown away.

Naïve he may have been, stupid he was not. He was a blank canvas and a fast learner. From that incident Vincent learned that his place was on the footpath. He made his way to South Main Street bridge and stopped to watch the water flow. He had only seen it at night when he was repairing the roof. The intrigue did not stop with the flame of the stove, Vincent longed to experience the rushing water. He climbed on top of the wall in order to jump into the river. As his second leg ascended to the top of the wall a passerby pulled on the straps of his raincoat.

"Jesus Christ, lad! What are ya doing? It's not worth it."

As the stranger pulled him back he grabbed a hold of Vincent's hand to stabilise him.

"Ah man, you're running a terrible fever, your hand is roasting! Are you hallucinating, like?"

Again, Vincent's first few steps in the real world were more error than trial, but this was yet another curve learned.

"Ah, no, no I am quite all right, thank you, sir. I just wished to look, but thank you." Vincent smiled at the stranger who cautiously walked away. The intrepid explorer continued to the far side of the bridge and roamed without care of direction or location. It would not be long before he was lost. The whole city glistened to him, it was one giant playground. The sights, the people, the sounds and the smells. His senses were alive and so was he.

After the threat of Gardaí, colourful language and following his forced removal from several shops, Vincent realised he was doing something wrong. He couldn't quite figure it out, but he had narrowed it down; somewhere between the point of picking up an item in the shop and the time he walked clean out the front door, he was doing something wrong.

Vincent decided to learn by observation. He walked along Washington Street where he followed a young lady into a convenience shop. She walked down to the fridges to pick up a bottle of orange. A not so subtle giant in a trench coat loomed over the magazine stand as he observed her every move. Once the young lady reached the top of the shop, Vincent realised the first flaw in his process, namely that you must go up to the man behind the counter. This intrigued Vincent. So much in fact that he lost what little sense of incognito he possessed. He barged up beside the woman who could feel her personal space being swarmed. As she curled her lips she looked at Vincent and then the very same eyes rolled at the cashier. She rummaged through her handbag.

"Ah, sorry, here's my purse."

As he stared at the flaps of brown that once belonged to a cow, he waited on tenterhooks. Finally it made sense, as the lady counted out the change on the counter, Vincent understood the concept of currency and barter, at least to some basic degree. He watched her place the purse back into her bag. As the lady sorted her belongings, Vincent's hands rose up vertically, elbows bowing at the sides. They plunged into his coat pockets: lint, paper, a phone number and a yellow faded letter to someone named 'Sarah'. No purse though.

He followed the lady out of the shop and stopped her a short while down the street.

"Excuse me, ma'am, I am sorry to bother you."

The lady was five foot four and Vincent towered a magnificent six foot eight. She didn't take much notice in the shop, but out on the street, he commanded attention. Despite the lack of trend in his clothing, Vincent's sheer good looks ensured that the young lady was by no means upset.

"No bother at all! Wow, you're a tall one, aren't you, boy?"

"Yes, I suppose my stature is greater than that of the observable population."

"Tall *and* a charmer! So what can I do for ya, lad?"

"I wish to know where I could acquire a purse?"

Good looks can carry quite a weight, but it is still only a certain weight.

"A purse!? What cha' mean a purse?"

"Yes, a purse. I wish to have one so that I can trade its contents for goods."

Vincent, it seemed, was almost like a savant. On this earth a little over two days and he spoke with better diction than most people he would ever meet. Yet still he could not decipher a male name from a female one. He repaired the building like an expert craftsman, yet understood virtually nothing about money. He was expert in some areas and amateur at others. It was as though he jarred half of the information out of his head when he fell from the clouds that night. Perhaps it would all come back to him in time. Perhaps he would have to learn it all again. Or maybe he would never fully know once more what he knew before the storm.

He was, at least, far beyond a fast learner. And from the facial expressions followed by the harsh words spoken in reply to his reason for wanting a purse, Vincent realised it was best to wait and ask John about such things.

John! In the excitement of the day's adventure, Vincent had completely forgotten that he was to be home for three p.m. Furthermore, he had no watch and even if he did, he was less than au fait at time telling. He wondered if asking passers-by the time would only earn him more instances like that of the purse pursuit. After a few moments of leaning towards people and half mumbling he went for it. It was two fifteen p.m., which Vincent was told was quite close to three p.m.

So no, time requests were not a problem. It was time to see how direction related questions were viewed.

"Excuse me, do you know the way back to John's home, please?" came the question leered to passers-by from a politely ignorant giant. It seemed that questions like this were responded to by people narrowing their eyes and replying in smart remarks. However, some people chortled 'that way and this way' with random directions pointed out. After following these malicious directions on a few occasions, Vincent realised that not everyone was genuine. This was to be a facet of earth that Vincent would struggle with most.

Back and forth across the city, he was becoming more and more stressed. He began to plead with passers-by and tell them that he 'wished to learn of John's address'. Again, most people ignored him until one snide remark came gleaming with a silver lining;

"Learn about John's address? What do I look like, a library?"

Library. He thought to himself that, if he could find this 'library', whatever that was, then perhaps he could find John's apartment. The stranger's remark came just in time, as Vincent was already contemplating shedding the coat and taking flight.

After asking for directions, Vincent found himself outside the grey stone of the library. Little did he know that John's apartment building was just over the bridge nearby. Being able to speak was something that Vincent remembered. Being able to read was something Vincent remembered. However, being quiet in a library did not fall into that category.

***

The clock glared down at John. It's aggressive face read five fifteen. By this stage he had stopped pacing, but he was by no means any calmer. As he sat on the couch he began to evaluate his situation once more. Had things really changed? He thought, that if anything, everything was back to normal. Three days ago he had no hole in his ceiling, he had no winged stranger in his life. As he sat there, alone, with ceiling intact once more, he asked himself what was different. Apart from the scorched veins of the bedroom floor, it was as if the last few days had not even happened.

Unfortunately, John had allowed himself to fall prey to something that affects all humans from time to time. He foolishly allowed himself to imagine what might have been. Like anything powerful, thoughts like this are also dangerous. Out in that lumberyard, he allowed his mind to wander down the avenues of Vincent-funded financial gain. He could find a way of leaving this terrible flat behind. But worse still than thoughts in the moment of what *might* be are thoughts of what *might have* been once the moment has passed. And beyond all the thoughts of money, was the realisation that John was no longer alone. This allowed him to imagine ways of leaving not just this terrible flat behind, but a terrible life. Once the floodgates of hope and ambition open, you are forever saturated with the wanting desperation that comes hand in hand. Thoughts such as this, of hope, are not for free. They come at a terrible cost.

Most of his time was spent plodding along, his encounter with Vincent was brief, but it was more important than the last few years of his life put together. As the second hand of the clock clambered above, John further resigned himself to the ever-changing reality. He thought worse still: now that he had no secret to keep who would believe him? Mrs O'Flaherty? What good was that, it was no good at all.

Before John sank the entire way through the couch and into the empty apartment below, he was jolted to his feet by the sound of the door buzzer. Nobody ever visited John and he knew it. It couldn't have been Mrs O'Flaherty, no, her style was more along the lines of shouting obscenities at the bedroom window. That meant only one thing. And just as you think that it was Vincent below, so too did John. He allowed the floodgates open once more. Hope is powerfully potent stuff, even the tiniest drop.

A second buzz and John swung the front door wide as he ran into the hall and descended stairs two and three at a time. He ground to a halt just before the final turn of the banister and continued in a calm and controlled swagger, as if to say that he hadn't been hanging on the arms of the clock.

There, at the end of the hallway, through frames of wood and glass, was the shape of a man. A rather tall man. From upstairs resonated the tone of a third buzz as the hand shadows outside matched the action. John glided to the blue release handle, the released chuck made the bolts of the front door click. Silence. There was still evening sun outside and some of it was brave enough to venture down this otherwise dark and dismal alley. The rays illuminated the shape of the man outside. The door opened casually.

"Hello, John. Sorry that I am late."

Quite literally two minutes of being nonchalant was all John could muster. Time enough to get back into the apartment. Then John reacted. It was less like a stranger harbouring a man from the clouds, and more like a parent who was scolding a child for walking the rail roads, all the worry and hurt was transformed into anger that they went at all. Just like parents, John was happy to see Vincent, although he certainly didn't show it.

"What the fucking fuck? What the fuck do you think you're playing at like? Jesus Christ, do I have spell *everything* out for you?"

Vincent stood motionless but with complete attention. He also stood silent.

"I mean it, Vincent, or whatever the fuck you're called! Where were you? Why did you leave the apartment? Like, does anyone know, huh, like, I hope you kept that coat on nice and cozy in the sun! I mean it, where did you go?"

There was not a single fibre of contempt stretched across Vincent's face, despite being scolded, he felt no manner of bad feelings towards John. He simply replied, but his speech had changed.

"As I said at the front door, John, I am sorry. I must be honest, within the first hour of you leaving I became bored and

I succumbed to the temptation of the city. I understand why you are upset and as I said, I am sorry."

Normally John was a man controlled by temper and, at times, conquered by it. But he could not argue with such honesty and sheer lack of will for confrontation.

"Well, am, okay then," spoke John, still stern, but faltering. "But, where did you go? And does anybody know about, well, the way you are, did you blow your cover? You know, fall through any buildings, that kind of thing?"

Vincent smirked. It was the first real emotion John had seen since the upset from his questions the previous night.

"No, John, I decided against such things," replied Vincent as his smirk became a smile. "I decided that I could no longer wait to see the city. It is amazing, John, the world outside the window."

"It's okay, Vincent. I guess it's not half bad in the sun. Where did you go all these hours, and where have you picked up the relaxed lingo, you get a massage or something?" asked John.

"I just walked. I walked and enjoyed every step. It did not take long before I began to realise that some places are safer to walk than others. I must admit to you, John, when a stranger told me the time was near your arrival home I began to feel worried. I was lost and I didn't know the name of your address. Luckily, a stranger who was less forth coming with aid informed me of the library. What a wondrous place it is John. I apologise once more for my late return, but once I started it was very difficult to stop indeed."

By the time Vincent finished speaking, it was not just John's accent that had an upwards inflection. By now his left eyebrow was high atop his forehead.

"What do you mean you 'couldn't stop'?"

"Reading, John. I couldn't stop or 'put the book down' as the lady who owned the library said. She was nice, once I learned how to speak in a whisper she was more than helpful. I must be further honest with you, John. I have not fully understood everything you have been speaking about since I arrived. So I started with the dictionary."

John's brow climbed higher. "What do you mean 'started with'?"

"I decided that the first book I should read was the dictionary, just so there would be no more confusion between us."

You would imagine that John was beyond the realm of question and disbelief. "So you mean to tell me that you read the dictionary, the whole thing?"

"Yes, John, all two-hundred and six-thousand, three-hundred and eighty-four words of it. From Aardvark to Zyzzyva…" Vincent smiled at the puzzled look on John's face and then continued "…it is a genus of tropical American weevil, found mainly in-"

"I know what it is!" shouted John. Once the outburst had passed John hoped Vincent would not ask him for Zyzzyva related facts because of course he had never heard of such a thing.

"Once I had finished the dictionary, I realised intellectual pursuit took precedence over literary pleasure, at least until I am more accustomed with this world. There is so much I do not know. I read several broad science books and explored every available atlas that was in stock. I finished with a map of Cork city, it was funny that the library on Grande Parade is only a short distance from here! I was only around the corner all that time I was in the library. I must go back, John. But it is not opened again until Monday."

John didn't know how to think. He certainly didn't know what to feel. At least when he was cross and worried he knew exactly what he was. After those last few moments he was a man without mood. He turned away and leaned on the counter. The brain can work in a flash. John realised he was reassured once more. Vincent was back and so too was all the hope that came chained with him. All he wanted to do was read and learn, at least for now. That was enough, it was time to think and time to plan. He turned back to Vincent.

"Don't worry, it's only a day away, tomorrow will come and go and before you know it you'll be buried in books."

"It is not just books, John, it is all that they hold, already there is so much that I now know I must see, so much to do."

"Yes, but, ah, before you do any of those things, you have to learn more. I mean, come on Vince, you're like an alien here. Sure you're probably smarter than most people already, but it's a mean world out there. There's a lot of street smarts that you can't get from a book. Don't worry, I'll watch out for you."

"Thank you, John. It was a good thing I found the library. I was ready to fly back to you, the city is a lot easier to-"

"Jesus Christ! So she really did see you? Vincent, I never asked you, but how did you fix the roof the other night?"

Developing fast and having a limitless brain is no match for a lifetime of human interaction. Selfish pursuits aside, there really was so much that Vincent needed to learn from John. The concept of lying was just such an example. Where others would have felt the stern bone of contention in John's voice, Vincent heard only an innocent question, one that he answered innocently.

"I waited until dark, so it was safe, and then I flew to–"

"No! Fuck it! Don't you get it, lad? It's never safe! It is never safe to fly, and I don't think it ever will be. Not... not until we sort this out."

Again, reality was met with innocence.

"But, John, I waited until it was dark, to ensure secrecy."

"No buts, Vincent! You can't risk it. *We* can't risk it. It's just too dangerous, like. No matter what, you can never fly. Do you understand me?"

Vincent stood sombre. Imagine the freedom that yearns inside us all. Imagine the ability to escape this earth. Imagine defying gravity by your own rules. Then imagine it is all stripped away. With one sentence, you are shackled to the soil. If you could truly imagine all this, then you would not be able to imagine Vincent accepting what John was demanding of him. And Vincent did accept it. Sombre as he may have been, he trusted John. Books cannot teach you the sting of mistrust. Not in an evening. Not in an eternity. Vincent would one day learn about this the same way all on Earth do, by feeling it in their own heart.

"Okay, John. If you think it is best." Vincent smiled in solidarity.

"I do, I really do. Don't worry, as far as I know Mrs O'Flavs is the only one who saw you. We'd be in more trouble if a seeing eye dog saw you, more people would believe the dog.

But trust me, buddy, just until we figure out a plan. I see great things for us, lad! Yeah, I can see it now! You and me all the way, Vince, you and me." John smiled at Vincent a more genuine smile than he had curved in years. "So, go on. Tell me some of the 'wonderful stuff' you learned."

**

And so for a short time, this was John's life. And for a time, life was good. During the day he would go to work and Vincent proceeded to make his way through the alphabet and indeed the breath of the library's resources. When Vincent realised that people were returning the books they had 'stolen' the previous week, he finally understood the full extent of how the library operated. However, he didn't understand it fully. The first day he decided to take books home was a sight to behold. Observation is important, but it is not everything. He did not know that one must be a member to check books out. And so, that first evening, Vincent paralleled his colossal thirst for knowledge with his mammoth strength. Rose, the librarian, had never seen so many books stacked so high. Entire volume sets and complete works sailed towards the exit in perfect balance and not a sweat was broken. Needless to say, she did not adhere to the whispering rule.

When John wasn't working he explored the city with Vincent. He never really looked at the city until he viewed it through Vincent's eyes. The mundane and everyday of a city in grey came to life with questions and the light of appreciation. Have you ever endured a rainstorm with someone who is still amazed by rain? Some people taste the rains and love the winds, some people simply get their clothes wet! Vincent revelled in what no passer by would even begin to notice; the drops of rain would evaporate from Vincent's face, his skin was still like that of a latent furnace, hot to the touch.

Having nothing or no one to compare to, Vincent had no real sense of humour of his own. So it did not take much to begin to adopt the one John had. He taught him words that were not in the dictionary and how to look at women on the bus without looking like a near seven-foot pervert. He taught him the stuff he needed to know and he tried his best to explain the grammatical inconsistencies of Cork colloquialisms;

"I don't understand, John, I asked him if he would allow me try one for free and he replied 'I will yeah!' I thought this was very nice of him. Then when I tried to leave without paying for it, the man became irate and snatched it back! Why would he say yes only to change his mind?"

"No, Vince. 'I will, yeah' means no. As in, it's like a form of sarcasm, ya know? Like, if you asked someone would they buy you a car, they might say 'I will, yeah' as if to say they'd do it when pigs fly, you know?"

Vincent didn't know. It was not the first time he fell vulnerable to the vernacular and it would not be the last.

After a very short ban, Rose the librarian allowed a bewildered giant to return to her library once more. But this time she asked to see his membership card and explained he could only take three books at once. He of course, had no such card.

"Right then, let's get you signed up. Name?"

"Vincent."

"And your surname Vincent?"

For all he had learned in such a short space of time, for all his magnificent intelligence, he simply could not think on his feet. Instead he simply continued to smile and hoped that the moment would pass. It didn't. Rose repeated herself.

"What's your last name, Vincent?"

"Just call me Vincent."

Rose laughed a little bit which was entirely out of her character "Well I can't very well call you Mr Vincent, now can I? So come now, I'm a busy woman."

Vincent whished so desperately that John had been with him. Only now did he realize that they should have thought of this sooner, it was only a matter of time until somebody asked after all. Vincent did his best to continue.

"I don't have one of those."

"Of *those*?" repeated Rose as she twisted her face, half in wonder and the other half in annoyance. Vincent realized that the situation was getting out of hand. John would not approve of such a spectacle. Then Vincent realized that they had made up his first name. Why so should there be any harm in doing the same with his second? He looked Rose straight in the eye and excused himself before saying, "VERNE! Yes, that's it. My surname is Verne."

"Vincent…*Verne?*"

"Yes, that is who I am."

Rose considered a thought for a moment and then continued "Interesting, any relation to the author?"

"No, not at all. I'm just rather fond of the name."

Rose was more curious than ever at the back of that comment but she had a library to run.

"Here you go, *Verne*, don't lose it now or I'll have to charge next time."

Vincent smiled at Rose and she smiled back. It felt nice.

***

The lumberyard was a cold job, even in the summer mornings. By now it was June, and in the month or so that had passed there was one thing that ran the tracks of John's mind and kept his focus from the bitter job at hand. It entered his mind before any other questions could enter. Perhaps it was not the most important, but to John it was the most pressing. Maybe because it was the easiest answered. It was not the question of Vincent's origins. It was not even the question of what was best done with Vincent – a question of which John was no closer to answering. No, for the mean time John was content in having a buddy, another bachelor for the pad.

The question that plagued his morning mind, was the extent of Vincent's abilities. What were they, and what were their limits? In order to make the best possible plan, John needed all the information he could get. He needed a way of testing Vincent and he needed a place to do it. But he had to be careful, what if it went too far, but John wasn't so sure that there was a too far. After all, he did fall from the heavens and his skin was near boiling half the time. John was no scientist, but he knew he must approach this with caution. The only way he knew of revealing the full extent of a ruler's full flexibility, was when it finally snapped. For an angel, this was not an option.

The echoing walls of the library held more than just knowledge, they held experience. There often is not much for adolescents to do. In the rain, there is even less. Contrary to popular belief, idle hands are not those of the devil. They belong to those left in the awkward limbo that a young person finds themselves snared in. This limbo is the desolate doldrums between being too old to play and too young to enjoy the finer things in life. But boredom does not begat destruction. If this was true so many problems could be sorted so easily. Destruction is borne from a young life that has been destroyed. It breeds all sorts. The dangerous minorities, the confused masses and then, then there are those who have never enjoyed anything and so it becomes their mission to deny enjoyment to others. Vincent was about to deal with this phenomenon first hand.

The great thing about a public library is that it is open to all. The downfall of a public library is that it is open to all. Ryan, Jack and Kevin were products of the failings of society. Actually, that is not entirely true. Jack and Kevin were, and for this they could be forgiven. But Ryan, he was one of those boys who came from a good home, equipped with good parents who only wanted the best for him. But instead he chose the allure of being degenerative and chose the life and friends he was lucky enough to have the choice to avoid. Kevin and Ryan were sixteen. Jack was seventeen, a fact that helped in the deciding of his dictatorship. The three boys would routinely come to the library and piss off Rose and the quiet alike until they were eventually moved on. These boys were by no means the scourge of the earth, but neither were they wallflowers. Vincent's soft nature made him an easy target.

Frequently, Vincent would reach for a book and one of the three would snatch it before him and pretend to read it, using their index finger to push imaginary glasses up the slopes of their nose. Sometimes they would take the book, other times they would simply drop it to the floor. Of all the wonders Vincent was encountering, this was one of the few that left him most confused. The boys mistook his dumbfounded air for fear and they revelled in it.

In the evenings, John showed Vincent how to cook the simple meals he enjoyed. Despite not needing the function, he loved to watch the matter change from ingredients into dinners. Eggs simply astonished him! The modest budget that John survived on thrived on the versatility of these shelled delights.

"Really? You mean to tell me you're *still* not hungry? Like, not even a bit?" John often wondered what Vincent ran on, what was his source of power, his energy?

In fact Vincent never ate for he was never hungry. Neither did he ever drink, it simply wasn't an issue. In fact, apart from the few articles of clothing that John had purchased in the charity shop, Vincent was no labour on his budget, not remotely. He never ate and he had no concept of frivolous spending. Neither had John, but that was because he was broke, he still had the desire. Vincent was content, in fact he was delighted with the simple pleasures he found among the pages and amidst the walls of the library and the views of the skies.

They would talk late into the night, Vincent rather enjoyed scrabble but after a week or two John realised there was no point even keeping score. He would regale Vincent with half-truths and whole lies about women who would flirt with him through the gates of the lumberyard. John may have thought Vincent an angel, but Vincent thought him a God. The concept of jokes was still a long way from being fully understood, but they were still enjoyed. As John whisked eggs into wine, Vincent would tell him what Jack and Kevin 'did next' and just how cross it made Rose. He even began to regale John in turn with reports of how he would help Rose move the boys along and her gratitude in return.

Yes, for a time, this was their life. It wasn't much, but it was theirs. But only for a time. Something as beautiful as friendship has an inherent fragility.

***

On both sides of the desk the books were stacked high. Vincent was making quick work of all works beginning with the letter 'j'. In lieu of his methodical technique, he could not avoid the tangents of his interests. Before he would know it, spines were bent doubled as the stacks would climb higher. But today was different. Despite the fact the books were for everyone, today there was a book just for Vincent. From around a looming tower came the equally immanent nose of the book fly, Rose. She peered along its ridge at the hunched giant. By now, he was well accustomed to this and knew exactly what it meant.

"Hello, Rose. I am being quite the book hog, aren't I? I'll put some of them back now."

"And while you're at it, *Verne*, call round to 'm'."

Vincent paused as he looked at his collection before him, his main focus was on 'J' and none of the side books were under 'm' either.

"Excuse me, Rose, but none of these books should be filed under 'm' unless of course the library has changed their system. In either case, I must admit that I am confused."

"Why on earth would we change the system like that? Just put those back and call around to 'm' on your way round, will ya?"

Doing as he was told, Vincent was overcome with a feeling of suspense that he had not felt before. After he correctly placed the last book in its correct slot, and fixed one or two rogues along the way, he arrived at section 'm'.

There, over six feet above the bottom shelf, protruded another rogue. Being about the only person tall enough to reach it without the stepladder, Vincent reached up and pulled it out, as if it had been left there for him and for him alone. This book didn't even begin with 'm' and seemed to be completely out of place. And then Vincent took more notice of the title; '*In Search of the Castaways*'. He had wanted this book two weeks ago. After approaching Rose and following a rather clumsy and convoluted conversation, he enquired into the mechanisms of ordering a book. Unfortunately, the library ordered books en mass every four to six months. He was told it would be at least another two months before the surveying and ordering would commence.

"Well, considering the rate that you're flying through these books, I just thought you'd have everything read by the time that book came." Spoke Rose as she stood at the end of the aisle. "Just make sure you don't hog that one too." Rose smiled the same smile that she had given Vincent on the day she issued his membership card. It made him feel warm inside like never before. All of a sudden his head was light and the book seemed heavy.

Vincent looked at her and then at the front cover of the book. It was a hard back, with a green, almost velvet cover, embroidered in gold stitch. As he looked to Rose his hand glided through the air, as if the weight of this book was the first thing he struggled to lift since he arrived. He continued to look at Rose.

"This is the most marvelous book in the building. I understand the term 'speechless' better than ever. Thank you, Rose."

And with a swipe the moment had gone. Enamored with the situation, the sensors in Vincent's hand responded unusually slowly, but it only took the next fraction of the very same second to realise what had happened. There, like a pack of coyotes, stood the boys with nothing better to do. Today there was two more than usual, but the core was there and in the middle of it all stood Kevin with the book in his hand.

"What the fuck is this one about, huh? Ha boys look at it! It's all shiny like a girl's book!"

Tolerant to this world and without a shred of aggression, Vincent calmly asked for the book back.

"Why do you want it back? Is it a gay book, ha, is that it, a book for fags like?"

Hysterically laughing at his own ingenious quips, Kevin was spurred on by the chorus of laughter bellowing from the other boys. By now they had drawn attention and Kevin was loving it. Rose was furious, but too intimidated to say or do anything much about it. Vincent was not used to this aspect of the world. Although he was not angry with the boys, he was beyond confused. He could not determine how such direct logic was being over ruled by sheer ignorance. More than anything, he simply did not understand what was happening.

"Please, I would very much appreciate you returning the book, it was a very nice act on Rose's behalf and-"

"Oooohhh!" chimed the group of boys. Kevin continued, "It's weird isn't it for your *girlfriend* to get ya a book for fags!"

"I am sorry, young man, but I'm afraid I really don't think you are making much sense. If you want the book that badly, by all means, I hope you enjoy it." Vincent truly meant what he said. Spurred on by their insatiable desire to rid themselves of boredom, the boys were getting little satisfaction here. They were getting no rise, no reaction, no conflict from Vincent. The book had lost its appeal.

"Ah fuck it, you're no fun, lad. Here, have your gay book back then."

Vincent reached out and smiled as he took the book with his left hand. And then, it happened.

A usual last resort used in order to get a reaction, was the technique of pretending to punch someone, just to see them flinch. It was just the kind of spineless, power hungry action that Kevin thrived on. As he turned away from Vincent he snapped back suddenly. He hurtled a punch towards Vincent, intending to stop his fist a few inches from Vincent's gut and revel when he flinched. But the outcome of this little stunt was to be very much different.

As his fist began to sail through the air, Vincent's reflexes got the better of him. With the intent of simply blocking the oncoming fist, Vincent's right arm sprung forward. His open hand fired vertically like a spear being launched. It rested stationary in the air with the back of his hand facing Kevin. It happened in a split second. The skin around Kevin's knuckles bent and warped around the few golden hairs on Vincent's hand. Then came the collision. As bone met bone, Vincent's hand did not falter. It was as if Kevin had punched a wall of solid titanium. The bones in his hand cracked before they split, then split before they shattered. As the wave of energy rippled towards his elbow, the recoil of his skin passed over his wrist as the skin around it split like dry rubber, unable to take the influx of fragments of bone. In a second, it was over.

Kevin's knees buckled under the force of the shock. He slumped sideways and slammed into the bookcase. He screeched a high pitch tone as he inhaled deeply, just before he let rip. He began to scream and wail as spit flew from his mouth and tears streamed down his cheeks. He slumped to his knees and then fell on his side, holding his hand. Behind him his friends backed away, before him, Vincent did the same. Vincent's heart was racing, he had coiled his right hand close to his chest and far away from the belief of what just happened. He mumbled apologies over and over. His hand ran from his chest up along his face and along towards the back of his head. His hand stained his beautiful golden hair with splatters of blood as it brushed through in an attempt to calm himself. He continued to back away as Kevin screamed ever louder on the floor. It was too much for Vincent to absorb.

He turned to run and knocked Rose clean off her feet, the shock of which made him release his left hand. The book hit the floor as hard as Rose. Vincent ran down the centre of the library, echoes of screams adorning the walls. He burst out onto the main street and sprinted for home.

John climbed to the top of the staircase to see his front door ajar. The light from the opening made shapes across the floor and up along the wall at obtuse angles.

"Vincent?" Spoke John as he pushed open the door. He looked into the sitting room, his housemate was nowhere to be seen. When he found his way to the centre of the room he looked through the doorframe of his bedroom and saw Vincent thrown down on the floor. His left arm was slapped across the inside of the window and his head rested atop his forearm. The room was dark except for the glow from the orange streetlight that bathed Vincent. John walked to the threshold of the room but no further.

"Buddy, what are you doing down there? Are you all right, like?"

John was genuinely concerned. He had never seen Vincent in such a repose. In fact, John was beyond concerned, he was a little unsettled. He tried again.

"Well, buddy, are you going to tell me? What's up with ya?"

And then John heard it, the sound of sobbing. Vincent wasn't just resting his head. He was crying. John left unsettled far behind and entered the realm of fear. John was experiencing the shock that humans feel when a constant they have grown to rely on fails them. Like a child who views their parents as titans among us, as beings of unlimited ability and complete security. When that parent is seen as mortal and human for the first time that stability in your soul cracks and splits from the top of your belief to the very bottom of your core. This is how John felt. He had grown accustomed to Vincent as some form of celestial being, free of human weakness. This completely offset his beliefs.

"Jesus Christ, Vincent, what happened, are you okay?"

There was no reply. John stooped down next to Vincent. He managed to raise his head from the depths of despair.

"I'm sorry, John, I'm sorry. I am so sorry. I didn't mean to hurt him. It was an accident, I am being honest, I am, I am, I promise I am sorry."

All spoken in the one breath, John could hear the pain in his voice. By the time he fully exhaled he broke down into tears and sank once more into his own arms. John was terrified.

"Vincent, what do you mean? What do you mean you are sorry, what did you do? Hurt who, Vincent, who did you hurt? Oh my god, oh my god. Who was it, Vincent, what did you do?"

John grabbed both sides of his head and pulled so that the two men faced each other. Panic was running rife.

"Vincent! Tell me, tell me what you did!"

Vincent recounted the situation in perfect detail. When he finished speaking, John let go of his head and he himself fell backwards against the wall and slid to the floor. In one way he was relieved, a part of him had thought that Vincent had killed someone. But another side of John feared the retribution for this act, no matter what the form, it was almost certain to blow their cover. As John joined Vincent in the pit of despair, the winged and crying giant turned to him. He calmed in order to ask a question.

"John, when I first came here you asked me was I an angel. I told you that I was unsure because I didn't even know what that was. It was the first word I looked up, John." He broke to sob. "Angel; noun: *one of a class of spiritual beings attendant upon God, a divine messenger from God, a guardian spirit who is kind, pure or beautiful.* Does what I have done sound like an Angel, John? Does it!"

There was not just pain in his voice, but anger. John became increasingly alarmed.

"Vincent, buddy, calm down. Listen, I'll tell you what I think what you told me sounds like. It sounds like an accident, Vince, that's all. To be honest, it sounds like it was more that guy's fault than yours, I mean. You would never do that on purpose."

Vincent continued to cry.

"But does it sound like something an angel would do? Does it?" John simply remained silent.

"Well then, if I am not an angel, then what am I, John? What am I? What am I even doing here?"

With that, Vincent dried his eyes and took to his feet. He walked out into the sitting room and made strides for the door. John called after him but Vincent ignored him as he walked out of the apartment. John ran after him, when he ran into the hallway he expected to see Vincent's head as he walked down the stairs, instead he saw the backs of his legs as Vincent made his way towards the roof. Vincent made it to the third floor apartment and continued up the stairs. He stopped before the roof access door. Upon trying the handle of the large metal door he discovered that it was locked. In his temper he tore the handle from its screws.

The rooftop was awash in the blue hue of a full moon. It was quiet up there, only the sound of the river nearby and the handle falling to the floor interrupted the calm. Then the silence was shattered as the access door was sheered from its hinges before the hinges split from the walls as the sound of torn and contorted metal wailed across the rooftop. The door bounced along the flat roof before its massive weight endowed it with sudden inertia as it ground to a halt. Vincent walked out into the view of a lunar neighbour. He threw the trench coat from his shoulders just as John joined him on the rooftop. His wings opened half way before John shouted.

"Vincent! Stop! What are you doing? Have you completely lost it?"

The summer moon illuminated the brilliant white of his wings. He turned to face John who spoke at him harshly, terrified of the consequences of Vincent's actions.

"I mean it Vincent, you need to calm down and stop–"

"Don't tell me what to do!"

John was speechless. Vincent had never spoken back, in fact, he had never voiced much of an opinion on anything. His voice was deep and powerful, he leaned in close so that both men were face to face. John could feel the heat from Vincent's skin; it was hotter than normal, much hotter. It was like the wave of heat from an oven door falling open. Vincent stood panting and in the periphery of his vision, John could see wings that were outstretching and rising. Vincent spoke an aggressive hush through closed and gritted teeth "All I've done is listen to you, John, but where were you today when I needed you?

Why didn't you warn me against such things? You can't take care of me, John. You can't even take care of yourself!"

Emotion chased emotion as John didn't know whether to feel insulted or terrified. He had never seen this side of Vincent who continued to lean closer to speak.

"Does *that* sound like something an angel would say?"

John was genuinely frightened. But he could see something in Vincent's eyes. Beyond the anger, and under the upset, was pain.

A moment of silence passed. Then, in a burst of energy, wings fired downwards and Vincent rose before John's eyes. He turned in the air like a diver falling in reverse. As the unsettled dirt and dust swarmed around John's eyes he watched Vincent fly away, turning into a silhouette against the moon.

John watched and followed his shape in the sky for a moment longer before he noticed something a few feet away. There, between the door and the trench coat, was one, single, white feather. He walked over and picked it up.

In the three months since his arrival, Vincent had not lost a single feather, not one was shed around the apartment. John held the feather in his hand. It was roasting. As he looked out over the city, a breeze ran across the rooftop. He looked down at his hand where the breeze danced around the feather. Suddenly it cooled and began to disintegrate into the same gold fragments John had seen before. When the breeze had left, John stood there alone, with a hand full of golden dust.

CHAPTER IV

APOCRYPHA

Have you ever had a dream that you were so certain was real, that you were waiting to wake up from reality? That your real life no longer seemed credible, seemed believable? How yesterday can be so foreign from the here and now. Have you ever woken in the middle of the night in the orange light of the lampshade or the blue of darkness and been unsure of what to believe? It is a feeling universal to all humans. To wake uncertain of that which you know best can be shattering. It is in those few waking seconds that you fall fast and it is only when you have distinguished truth from mystery that you come crashing back to earth. Those seconds can be an eternity or they can be an escape, whichever it is depends on the life you lead outside your dreams.

***

John awoke several times that night, each time confused about realities. He was too cold without the blankets and too warm beneath them. Tossing did less good than turning, although both were extensively investigated. He was too tired to sit and too awake to lie down. He was a man in limbo, limbo of the mind, unsure if he should go back to the roof or stay as he was.

He had already been back to the roof twice that night, both times convinced he heard the thud of rooftop footsteps crunching gravel beneath. Both times he was wrong.

He could feel the draft find its way downstairs. Quiet like a jewel thief, it continued to sneak under the door and tickle John's feet. Intermittently, he would close his eyes and jam the cogs of his mind long enough to get some sleep. At best he would get twenty to twenty-five minutes. The shorter his sleep, the greater his confusion when he woke. For a man who had spent the last five hours in bed, John was exhausted.

Four minutes, that was all it took, but in four minutes John fell into a dream that was more real than the life he was living. The mind does not need time to know what it truly desires. John jolted awake for the ninth time that night. Wide eyes, his heart was panicking in his chest, the cold sweat running marathons down his face. The bed was freezing and he was on fire. The panic came from the storm that raged in his mind. For when he woke, he woke to the decision of discerning realities. Looking at the ceiling was of little use, it told him nothing, only that he was inside. And then he saw it, and although it was not the reality he was hoping for, his heart was able to relax in the knowledge that he at least had his answer.

The answer came atop his bedside locker.

They say it is the not knowing that is the worst. People say that they don't care what the answer is, they just want to know. Then, when the outcome is not the one they wished for, the very same people will claim that ignorance is bliss.

As John stared at the bedside locker, drenched in the sweaty bed sheets of which he only had one pair, he was ignorant of nothing. There before him sat a jam jar, absent of jam, but full of something sweeter; the truth. When John felt that feather bake and cool as it turned to dust in his hand, he made a fist around it, a fist to preserve something that even he struggled to believe. The most important thing in his entire possession was inside a tightly clasped jam jar, the base of which was thinly coated with the golden dust. He picked up the jar and held it close to his chest. The glass was like ice, greedy for the heat from his skin. With the jar pressed tightly against his body, John was able to fall asleep properly for the first time, safe in the knowledge that he would at least know the exact reality to which he woke the very moment he would wake.

A few hours later he awoke, the glass almost molten, but it had done its job. He quickly dressed and checked the time. Unlike most of his possessions, his watch was nice. It wasn't expensive or rare, but it was old and that gave it character. It also didn't work. It had been broken for the past four years, almost half the length of time he owned it. He kept a cheap digital watch in his pocket for function. But the broken watch that he wore on his wrist, John did not look at that for the time of day. He looked at it to remind him of a time when things were good. It reminded him of a time less lonely.

He was up early and so he made his way to the hall. What was usually a chilly hallway was now a deathly one, the cold breeze had settled in the walls all night. But where there are winds there is change and, cold as it may have been, it smelled fresh for the first time since he moved in. It was to be a wasted climb. He didn't know what he expected. Maybe that Vincent had returned in the night and was too embarrassed or confused to come back downstairs. There was nothing on the roof except a door and a few hinges that had gone awry.

The next day, when John bought the paper, the headline on page four caught his attention. 'Cork Boy Hits Hardback' John knew exactly what it was about. As he sat on the bus ride home from work, he crumpled the paper over and leaned deep into the pages. His heart was racing. What was it going to say about Vincent? Furthermore, what would people believe? The article began and continued fairly close to the story Vincent had relayed to John, along with the usual embellishment that sells stories. Then came the divergence.

'The seventeen-year-old, know as Kevin Ryan, told the Cork Reporter that he had been joking with the stranger described. He then states that the man turned on him without provocation and 'tried to grab him'. Frightened, Kevin went to defend himself by pushing the stranger away, while his friends called for help. Kevin then reports that the stranger, who he believed had been drinking, proceeded to punch him. In an attempt to protect himself, the young boy then shielded his head and face with his hands. This was when the stranger struck his left hand, smashing the bones inside.

'The boy was rushed by ambulance to Cork University Hospital. However, a member of the responding medical team, who wishes to remain anonymous for legal reasons, has informed this paper that the injuries sustained are not indicative of those received by means of a punch. The staff member claims that they are more consistent with 'being crushed or with someone hitting a concrete wall full force.

'Kevin Ryan maintains that his injuries were indeed sustained by the stranger. Unfortunately, there were no other members of the public present in the rear of the library when the incident occurred. Gardaí are continuing the investigation and treating it as suspicious.'

But there were others. Five witnesses, apart from Kevin's entourage, saw Vincent shatter that young boy's hand. But they were the very same people that so often had their solitude interrupted by threats, despite doing their upmost to avoid eye contact. Idle or otherwise, those threats left impressions of fear and unrest. Despite the diameter, the wheel always turns. When Gardaí arrived to a disrupted library, they began to question those who stayed behind. Collectively, they all told lies, instinctively none would stand up for Kevin. But, off the record, they had all seen it, they didn't know exactly what they saw, nor could they explain it. Equally so, none of them truly cared and no more was ever thought about it again.

John was relieved when he read the article in full. It wasn't ideal, but it also wasn't a front-page photograph of Vincent flying over the city with a crucifix in hand. But the article gave him an idea and with tomorrow off, John knew exactly where he was going.

She worried around her station with the exact same mannerisms as Vincent had described. Her hair was brown and large in both length and volume. Through it, ran silver hairs like lightning down tree bark, along with the two inch think frames that adorned her nose, adding years beyond her age. She looked as though she were constantly agitated, as if time working in a library had not yet acclimatised her to the fact that people did not put books back where they belonged, and that they never would. She was a woman in her early thirties, but her true age was almost impossible to establish from neither sight nor sound. John did not have to ask her name, he knew he was looking at Rose from Vincent's descriptions. But it is not always polite to be practical.

"Excuse me, I'm looking for a woman by the name of Rose, do you know where she is?"

Rose huffed and narrowed her eyes.

"Firstly, I'm sure you're looking for a *lady* and not a *woman*, secondly, I am her and thirdly you'll have to lower your voice if you wish to continue speaking with me."

They both paused above the rustle of distant pages and the orchestra of morning coughing. She raised her eyebrows sharply as if to say that she was waiting, but not for long.

"Sorry." They raised higher. Then John spoke softer.

"Sorry again. Look, I don't mean to bother you, but I'm looking for my, well, for my friend. I was wondering if maybe he'd been here. He hasn't been around since the start of the week, tall guy, very tall guy actually. Brown trench coat, quiet, reads a *lot* of books, kinda looks like—"

"Vincent."

"Yeah, actually he looks exactly like Vincent." John smirked an awkward smile after an uncharming comment. "Anyway, have you seen him around?"

Rose looked even more worried than usual. She moved a few books from the counter onto the return trolley and then back again. She turned to look at John.

"I don't know what to tell you. Being honest with you, I wasn't entirely sure what I saw. It didn't make sense. But I do know that yesterday when I was putting a book back on the tall shelves back there that I found…"

Rose paused and swallowed the moment. She turned to glare a deadpan stare at John.

"...I found a fragment of bone up there among the books. Among *my* books. But I also know that little bollocks had it coming and that Vincent was more frightened than any of us. But I'll tell you this much, I wasn't afraid of him, not really."

John didn't know what to say. What do you say?

"No, I haven't seen him since. I have a lot of work to do, excuse me."

After lunch, John rummaged around his tool drawer and found two miss-matching hinges along with screws of variable length and made his way to the roof, screwdriver in hand. The evening sun was more inviting than the work of fixing the rooftop door. He sat on the edge of the building. Facing the river, John surveyed a golden city, enjoying another rare day of sunshine. As he looked out towards the horizon, he wondered where Vincent was, it had been four days and he had still not come back. John wondered if he would ever be back. He lay backwards to rest and stare deep into the sky. Where in the city was he? That is to say, if he was even still here. John laughed under his breath when he realised that, if he could fly, he wouldn't stick around either.

Dozing through the hours, John awoke to a chilled breeze driving a vanilla sky. His joints creaked as his bones lumbered while his muscles laboured to bring him to his feet. He walked over to the metal door, still bent from where Vincent struck it from its hinges. The door lay on its bend, with the concave face looking at John. As he struggled to flip the door, its weight reminded him of Vincent's strength. Once over turned, he stomped the door back into as best a shape as he could. It took him nearly forty minutes to repair what Vincent had done in under four seconds, with 'repair' being a liberal term. Still a little crooked on its hinges, John looked at the skyline once more before pulling the door shut as best he could, having to slam it several times before finally wedging it into the frame.

Six days. It was six days in total that John spent wondering where Vincent had gone and if he would ever return. Then, at some time past six in the morning, the creak from the rooftop door woke John from his slumber, the jam jar rolled from his chest to the floor. John no longer wondered about Vincent's return. What he wanted to know now was if he was still angry.

***

Frozen between decisions, John also stood frozen in his room. To the right was his bedroom door, to the left his window. He looked out that orange stained glass he knew so well to see the early morning drizzle throwing tantrums against the glass. Through the door and into to his right ear sneaked the sound of a creaking staircase. John questioned what he was doing, he knew Vincent would never hurt him, he wouldn't hurt a fly. Sure, he might crush one of those fly's tiny legs in a library, but only by accident.

John walked out of his bedroom to the sound of a silent hallway that echoed across the other side of the far door. He decided that there was no reason in being afraid, fear would do him no good. Even if Vincent was here to hurt him, John knew that there was no way of resisting. He dropped the burglar routine and just walked to the front door as if he were casually walking to the bathroom. As the door opened inwards John had forgotten just how massive Vincent really was. He stood there, wings folded high above his shoulders, his golden hair saturated and, as usual, his skin was already beginning to boil the rainwater into steam. Vincent bowed his head in apology but both men stayed silent. John opened the door wide and stood at its side.

The two men stood listening to the songs of the kettle. Still in his boxers, John walked back to his room.

"I'm sorry, John."

John paused hunched over in the other room, unsure of what to say in return or how to say it.

"I'm sorry for leaving and I apologise if my actions scared you on the roof."

"I know you are, and it's all right, lad, I know you're sorry, I accept your apology."

But these words were mechanical and forced, a silence lingered for but a second before John asked the natural question which he most wanted to know.

"Where did you go, Vince?"

Vincent knew the true nature of this question.

"Don't worry, John, I was seen by no one. I am sorry for scaring you that night, if I am to be honest with you, John, I too was scared. I do not know what came over me. When I flew away into the night, I just wanted to get far away. When I was disrespectful towards you on the roof, I saw the same look in your eye that I saw on that young boy's face. It was like looking into the flame beneath your boiling pot, it was fear and it was burning. I had to get away from people. I flew high above the city. I flew until there were no more house lights, no more street lamps. I flew until I was over dark trees. There I landed, and I stayed deep in a forest and far from sight."

Vincent sounded different. John couldn't quite explain it but he knew he was not the same as when he left. He spoke like a man who was losing his innocence. He thought this because John knew exactly how that felt. Something happened out there, something had changed in him.

"I'll be honest with ya, buddy, ya scared me up there, not for long, but in that second before you took off. I was worried about you, not that you'd get hurt but, just – ah, man – it's not nice in here, but compared to out there, the world beyond these walls, the real world... just, I was worried was all." John scratched the back of his head as he looked away awkwardly. Even though he was delighted his friend had returned, his nature simply would not allow him to show it. He continued:

"I didn't think you were coming back, like. What happened out there, what did you do?"

"That night, the night I left, I was unable to calm down. I wandered around the woods, unsure of what I felt, unsure of what exactly it was that I was feeling. For the first time, John, I really understood that I was not of this world. Soon after, it began to rain, lightly at first and then the downpour came. I walked and then waded through woods and wind as the earth turned liquid beneath my feet, I walked for hours. I was unable to calm, John, I felt like I was never going to feel anything else ever again. As the moon made its way across the sky, shining down between the clouds it began to sink in the sky as the night time faded into light. I felt as though my heart were about to burst. I could not move past the feeling of not belonging. I breathed in deep, the smell of the trees filled my lungs and then I took flight."

Vincent's eyes were now closed and his head began to tilt back as he recounted his experience. By now he was completely dry, all of the rainwater had evaporated from his skin, which was spotless, and from his clothes, which were filthy.

"What do you mean, where did you fly?" asked John, nervous still of blown covers and escaped secrets.

"Up, John, I flew upwards. I flew straight up into the sky. I flew with all my strength, determined to leave this Earth behind. I flew faster and faster into the ever-approaching morning. I flew until the forest beneath was just a shrub and the city a ball of light. I flew higher still until the country spread vast beneath me until I could see the twilight shimmer on distant waves. I felt free, John. I felt as if I were leaving it behind. As I flew faster into the rain it felt as if it were gaining speed and weight. The drops came crashing against my face as I streamed through the clouds, they felt like pellets of lead. The wind raged and I could hear nothing from the earth below. I burst through the grey of the clouds into the sky between morning and night, fragments of ice parting as I flew solitary past. As I climbed higher the air grew colder, sharper. The rainwater on my clothes and wings began to freeze and crack as I worked ever harder in air that was ever thinning.

"By now my wings were working furiously to carry me just slightly higher, I felt as if someone had tied a rope to my ankles and had decided upon my capture. There, high above the clouds, the blue of the night was ushered out by the vast expanse of light flooding across the sky as the sun broke the horizon. The curve of golden radiation washed in time across the curve of my eyes and for a moment I believed I would make it. It was there that I drew my last waking breath and I knew for the first time what it was to feel the force of exhaustion. My wings beat one last time, my arms outstretched upwards. The damp of my feathers made them almost solid with ice and the weight of the world pulled on the frost of my back."

"Then what?"

"I fell. I just remember leaving the golden sky and falling back into the dark and rainy clouds. I don't know how high I got or how far I fell. I just know that it was not high enough."

"But what happened, where did you fall like, did you wake up in the air?"

"When I awoke the rain had stopped and the day was bright. I was somewhere on the outskirts of the woods in which I sought refuge. I don't know what time of day it was and I was lying in a crater of earth and fallen trees. It seems the earth is no better at absorbing crash landings than this building. I lay down there for some time. I was not disorientated, I knew exactly what had happened."

"Why we're you lying there then, Vince?"

"Because it was gone, John. It was gone and I was grateful. The feeling that I was trying to outrun had left me. At first I lay there to simply enjoy the feeling, to savour it. But then I lay there to think. I realised that, as much as I was not of this world, as different as I may be, for some reason or another I have been sent here. Either to be punished or rewarded or some uknown reason found somewhere between. But irrespective of why and how I have come to be here, the fact remains: I am here. And there is no escaping it. Then I heard the rustle of people in the distance. As I climbed out of the crater I found my way deep into the woods once more. During my time among the branches, something occurred to me. You know, John, with all that I have read and memorised since I arrived here, I have *learned* so very little. Out there, I realised that the incident in the library could not happen again. But over time, I came to understand that perhaps it is unavoidable. And that if something like that did happen again, I couldn't go making craters every time. So I stayed out there, until I realised that the first time I woke up after falling from the sky was a lot easier when I awoke in your home. It was easier to wake to a helping hand." Vincent smiled appreciatively at John before continuing.

"John, I may never fully understand what I am or where I am from, but I know that I need your help if I am going to stay here and figure out my purpose. Isn't that what people do, John, figure out their purpose?"

John laughed the laugh that a parent would produce when asked a simple question about life.

"I guess it is, Vince, at least we try to. But I think you're an exception, things aren't going to be the same for you."

"I know you think I am an angel, John, or some other heavenly body, but if I am going to stay here, I am going to have to start living like a human. And I am going to need you. Whatever my purpose is on Earth it involves you, it must, it simply must, why else would I have been sent to you?"

John walked out of the sitting room and into his bedroom. When he returned he had the trench coat in hand. He smiled as he handed it to Vincent. Vincent put it back on immediately and looked delighted to have such an article returned to him. As he fixed it around the shoulders and pulled his wings tightly against his back, the smile ran free of John's face.

"And, you're sure nothing else happened, like? Nothing out there or, you didn't leave the forest or anything, no?"

Vincent looked puzzled by John's question.

"I only ask because, well..." John looked at the floor and rubbed the back of his head. "...ah, man, it's just that you're completely different, like. I mean, you're not, you're still you like, but you just seem... you just seem like someone who's been gone for a year of deep thought, not a week. Are you sure nothing else happened?"

Vincent finished fixing his coat and looked at the floor as he did so.

"No, John, nothing else happened out there."

***

Over the next few weeks, John and Vincent's friendship began to blossom. Despite his abilities and the wings that grew from his back, Vincent began to become much more like a regular person after returning from the forest. And as time progressed, he became more and more natural in his persona.

He still went to the library on most days, he even began to strike up conversations with strangers and attended the book club meetings, although he was usually slow to contribute. Kevin never did come back to the library, neither did any of his gang. But unfortunately, Rose might as well have never returned either. She no longer spoke to Vincent. The first day he returned, she froze in the middle of her worried stride. She stared him square in the eye, a stare that said everything that needed to be said. It was a look that made Vincent want to fall into the deepest crater he could imagine, but he knew this was no longer an option. He went to speak. She turned away. He released whatever sentiment he had in mind as a belated breath and the two never made eye contact again. Vincent had lost his first friend.

The everyday was an adventure. It is so unusual to say that everything was back to normal, when 'normal' for John had only been a few months of his life, and had contained the actions of an angel. Nevertheless, John was happy with the arrangement, as was Vincent, and the two would become inseparable. He had now been on this earth nearly five months, and in all that time Vincent had never once eaten a single meal nor tasted a morsel. He simply never grew hungry. But, in his ever-stretching strides to become human, he decided that it was time he had his first bite to eat. What do you choose when you have never experienced the joy of food. Where do you start? John wasn't even sure that he was meant to eat, after all, if he never got hungry, was Vincent's system equipped to deal with such a fine tuned balance.

As they perused the menus of the world in their minds, they listed meal and treat alike. John wanted to avoid something large for two reasons; for starters, they were broke, so the pan-fried crab salads Vincent had read about didn't really fit their budgetary constraints. Secondly, if Vincent's bowls really didn't work, John did not fancy the idea of bringing him to hospital for a stomach pump.

Clear in his mind he could see the black blue x-ray of folded wings that they would surely discover. He could hear the doctor now; "Yes, we have the results, your friend seems to be both an angel and severely constipated." It was hardly the glorious world debut that John had in mind.

Upon asking Vincent if he was built to consume food he was met with the reply of shrugged shoulders and a grin saying 'you know as much as I'. With this in mind, they decided on something small, a snack, just to be cautious. They sat rooftop one evening, John looked on as Vincent had a repertoire of hors d'oeuvres listed that was ever growing. Enough was enough, and as Vincent sat listing the list John took to his feet and told him to stay put. He walked out of the building and down to the corner shop below. A few minutes later he returned with what was as good as gold, hidden in purple wrapping. John held out to Vincent a Cadbury's milk chocolate bar.

"Well go on, take it! I've had enough of this food listing, besides wrecking my head, it's making my stomach rumble nonstop."

Vincent looked at the bar as if it was from another world. In many ways, it was. He had seen these in shops on numerous occasions, but one had never been his own. He looked up at John and lifted his hand towards the bar. As his fingers clamped one end, John released the other. Vincent dropped his hand, as if struggling beneath the weight of the bar.

He composed himself and swung the cocoa present around to meet the grasp of his other hand. He treated the situation as if Prometheus himself were handing him down the very fires from Olympus. He removed the purple paper and crumpled it in his hand before placing it in his pocket. The shimmer of the golden foil ran across his eyes. It almost made the sound of sword on stone as the light cut across his face.

He punctured the foil and felt the chalky, chocolate surface, running his thumb over the squares as though in desperate search of Braille.

"Ah for God sake! You have bloody wings, like! You can't be amazed by a fecking bar of chocolate!" John laughed as Vincent was lost between the squares.

"Oh my God, look, you're probably going to live forever, but some of us are food for worms, so if you wouldn't mind..."

Vincent broke two squares from the body of the bar and then split the pair free of each other. The moment the first square split between the force of closing teeth, Vincent felt as if he was falling through the roof once more. His eyes shone and he broke into a resounding chorus of laughter. Chocolate, it seemed, was a good first meal.

From this point on, there was no stopping Vincent. Everything and anything was on the menu. The whole world had to be tasted. If integration was the goal then he was doing it like a professional, for Vincent soon succumbed to love the humble potato. He was astounded by variety that could be found in such a small plant. He loved them and he loved them every way imaginable. Baked and boiled were safe, yet delicious. John would arrive home to pots disfigured from relentless mashing of powdered spuds. Fried and scalloped and chopped into chips, Vincent could find no end to his insatiable quest for satisfaction.

However, this newfound passion for satiation created a problem for John. Before, when Vincent was content with rambling from bookcase to bureau, it was to no detriment of the purse strings. Unfortunately, with Vincent's pursuit of a real life, they both faced strangulation if the strings tightened anymore. The back of John's mind was still fast at work trying to best discover a way to make money off of Vincent. But as Vincent had not yet expressed want for a better life, John did not feel the pressure. But he would have to do something soon. John was caught in a strange no man's land; on one hand he feared that Vincent would be taken from him before John ever saw a penny and on the other, he simply feared losing the only company he had known for years. Until that time, John didn't much like the alternative, but ready or not Vincent was going to have to find a job. But little did John know, the job would find Vincent first.

***

A rut, by very definition, is something that one can very easily get stuck in. Stay in it long enough and that crevasse in which you live your life starts to become duller by the day. Before long, life in a rut begins to behave like the summer evenings that fast approach autumn. The light that flows into the opening of the hole in which you survive begins to slow to a trickle, lasting fewer and fewer hours every day. And as you sink deeper into the ground the openings through which you once fell shrink into cracks that allow only the thinnest slivers of light to enter. Patience turns ruts into tombs.

Before Vincent arrived, John had one foot in his tomb. Despite being a relatively young man in his late twenties, he was years beyond his age, both physically and in terms of being exhausted with life. When people drift into an unwanted solitary life, their bones begin to age beyond their years. These people become slow to move and even slower to change, until one day, they wake up to a life that is little more than an existence. He had become set in his ways, especially since his watch stopped working, or at least that was what he thought.

And as time progressed he became less and less adventurous. This continued until such time that the only places outside of work and home that John would frequent, was the nearby supermarket and an old man's bar. It was a bar sparsely filled with men of the sea who had never stepped a foot off of dry land. It was a refuge for those who had lost everything and for those who never had anything to lose. It was not the kind of establishment where you made friends. Nor was it one that would lend itself to acquaintances. It was a place where men sat in solitude and drank themselves deeper into depression, closer to death and further from everything else. It was a place to dwell in lonely company. John was the youngest man by far to frequent its doors.

But since Vincent had become a mainstay in his life, John no longer had use for the dying batteries that sat high on bar stools. Vincent symbolised an opportunity for a second chance. A chance that John was going to take. And so it was decided, budgets be damned – the two men were going to a pub for a drink. A nice pub, one with real people.

Despite his excitement, John was still nervous. This was a scene that he had not been familiar with for quite some time. The prospect of going out on a Friday or Saturday was somewhat daunting for him. In this case, Thursday night seemed like a good way to ease back into the scene. When John returned from work Vincent had cleaned his clothes as directed by John. Vincent still only had a handful of clothes, partly due to the lack of funds and partly to the fact that he was a colossus with wings. But nonetheless, he washed his finest earthly apparel and was ready to hit the town when John arrived home. John never had mechanical means of drying his clothes; he used to dry them by the fire or on the radiator. But now, the two men had a new system. When Vincent had the clothes washed, he would simply put them on for twenty minutes or so and his skin would evaporate them bone dry and wrinkle free.

This worked fine, until John realized that he never saw his underwear on the radiator. Surely Vincent knew that there was an exception for underwear? Surely.

While wrapped in the hysteria of excitement, John burst in from work and turned the radio up full blast. He began to dance around the apartment as Vincent stood there like a statue considering coming to life.

"Come on, man! We're hitting that TOWN tonight!"

Very quickly, John remembered that this was not going be like he was anticipating. Vincent was most likely going to knock someone over with his wings as he attempted to dance, with quite a high chance of killing them in the process. John didn't care though, nothing was going to bring him down, not tonight. Against the backdrop of the radio, he tried to budge Vincent from rigid into fluid, he gave up and danced solo into his bedroom. A quick change of clothes and they were to be off. As John sat on the bed changing his socks he sang along with the music in the other room. Just then his voice trailed and his mood sank. As the right sock balanced over his toes he lost the energy of the moment as he looked at his bedside table. It was the jar of golden dust. And it was no longer golden.

As the tune from the radio faded into the background, John stretched across the blankets and looked deep into the jar. Where fine dust was once spread across the base of the jar there was now sprawling crystals of red and brown. Memory could not serve him, for he did not know when he truly last looked upon the dust. Having grown accustomed to it, John no longer had need to look at it. He had stopped noticing it and merely remembered that it sat next to his bed. Therefore, it may have been changing colour over the last month, or equally, it may have turned in the very minutes that just passed, he would never know. On picking up the jar he could see that the crystals had fused with glass, even when inverted, they stuck to the base of the jar.

John had never told Vincent about the feather or the dust, he pondered the ramifications should he have done so. As he lay there, now considering the very same concern, Vincent walked in.

"What is this, John?" As Vincent took the jar from his hand it was clear that he knew even less than John did.

"Ah, that's ah, that's just jam that's after going bad. It gets like that if too much air gets at it."

Now was not the time, tonight was not the night.

"Come on, let me throw on my shoes and let's hit the town," said John.

They went to the Rockford, a bar in the centre of town. On the journey in, Vincent bombarded John with questions. What to do, what to say and who to talk to. He did not want to admit it, but John was just as naïve as the man from the clouds and he knew it. John couldn't remember the last time he kissed a woman that wasn't intoxicated and could barely remember the few that were. Vincent, for all that he was, was like a child in many ways. And the prospect of women both terrified and fascinated him. In these respects he was like any man on earth. He did not know the throws of passion, but before long, Vincent would succumb to the depths of wanting despair. It would be a fall further than any he'd yet experienced and deliver him to a crater from which he would never fully return.

In the face of his nerves, John had over looked something that he could not believe he had not taken into account. He had no idea how Vincent would respond to alcohol. As they neared the bar he questioned whether or not it would be a good idea for him to drink tonight. But for all his ways, and for all that he was, one thing he was not was a child. John thought it pitiful at times, that a being of such power so willfully took orders from John, a failure. But no more, no more of that life for either of them. John decided that tonight they were leaving lives behind them, leaving them to settle in the dust. Tonight, they were going to have fun, one drink wouldn't do any harm.

The gallant bravery soon shriveled as both men sat in the corner of the bar; now that they were there they were terrified of interaction. Both men sat with black pints before them, bubbling tiny streams of gas towards the creamy surface. As the bar began to fill, Vincent continued to ask questions. They were questions that John had no answers for, but that did not stop him. Before long a group of women descended upon the bar stools and Vincent was awash with fascination.

"And, tell me, John, how is it that I should greet a lady like the ones over there?"

Vincent still struggled with the concept of subtlety, as his powerful arm out-stretched a pointing finger. John slapped his hand down.

"Well, for starters, man, you have to play it cool, you know. You don't fucking poke their eyes out from across the room anyway, that's for sure. Pretend like you're not interested in them."

"But, we *are* interested in them, John."

"I know we are Vince, beggars can't be choosers! But that's why I said pretend! Another thing, you can't be too nice to them either, girls don't like that. They say they want a nice guy but they prefer fellas that treat them like shit. Like the saying goes, treat 'em mean, keep 'em keen."

A profound sense of confusion avalanched down Vincent's face.

"But, John, that doesn't make any sense. I am sorry, but I don't understand."

"It's okay, Vince, you're not meant to. Right, the next thing you have to remember is that you are a hunter, right?"

"A *hunter?*"

"Yes, a hunter! And there are always more hunters than deer. You have to get in there and scope out the woman before anyone else gets there."

"And then she is mine?"

"No, and don't say it like that, Vince, you sound like a weirdo."

"I'm sorry, John, I just find this all very backwards to everything else I have learned."

By this stage the bar had begun to jostle and the group of women had noticed Vincent.

"Look, Vince, yes, you have to get there first, but that's not the end of it. In fact it's the start. Then you have to mark your territory."

Vincent was shocked and John knew exactly what was going through his head, he decided to nip that thought in the bud before they really had a problem on their hands.

"No, Vince, don't even think about it, I mean it as a figure of speech, I don't mean you literally pee on the girl!"

"Then you should be more careful with your words, John."

"Okay, okay. But what I mean is that, even when you're talking to her, other guys will come up and try to steal her."

Then silence. There was a silence of terror as the group of women interrupted the two men.

"Hey, guys, how're ye keeping?"

Nothing, no reply, not a single word escaped their lips.

"So, are these seats taken or what?"

And as four girls sat down around the men, it was already the best night out John had had in a very long time. For you see, Vincent was quite possibly the most handsome man on the entire planet. His golden hair was thick in sprawling locks that adorned his tanned skin. His sheer stature and physique that found its way through the clothes detracted attention away from the trench coat he wore. His chiseled good looks meant that he would never sit alone. Luckily, in the excitement, Vincent forgot all the advice that John had given him.

This was not a bus stop, it was not a meeting, the girls couldn't care less about how socially inept Vincent was. In fact, because of his good looks they found his naivety cute and charming. Of course, the reality was that they didn't care if he was drooling. John knew what was happening and he didn't care one bit, for he was enjoying himself. When one of the girls realised that, geographically, she had picked the worst position to flirt with the golden stranger she resigned herself to this and continued to chat away with John. Beggers can't be choosers.

As the evening grew late and the drink continued to flow so too did the conversation. Just as Vincent enjoyed the sweetness of chocolate he began to fall under the caressing hand of alcohol. Despite enjoying themselves, neither man had any intentions beyond the table, John was not drunk enough to escape years of nerves and inhibitions and Vincent, well, Vincent simply didn't have a clue.

And then Vincent was to have his first taste of desire and it was every bite delicious. There, like a lone star at night on a wooden stool by the bar, sat a girl in her early twenties. It was the first time that Vincent was ever drawn towards a woman and what fantastic taste he had. She was splendid from head to toe and all that there was in between, not that that was very much at all.

Her skin was pale and smooth as though fire borne from porcelain but soft to the touch like ivory wrought in a dusting of chalk powder. Her lips were red from painted blood and looked as though she would taste to kiss of raspberries. She folded, neatly beneath her slender body, legs that had all the shapes of being cut from ice and fashioned in glass. Her curves fit the right proportions like a mannequin cast of pure imagination. Black hair danced across her forehead and spilled like oil about her shoulders as it starkly broke the contrast of her ivory skin. Blue eyes that had not yet been dulled by the broken promises of the realities of life sat like precious stones as though they were the prize of her face. They glittered with delight and want-full expectation that comes from the carefree naivety and bliss of a commitment free existence. She was the very spoils of nature, wrapped as danger in stunning flesh and bone.

The chatter of John and the girls around faded into a haze and hushed about his ears. Without warning or thought Vincent rose from the table and walked straight over to her. Of course, he had no plan, but neither was there an ulterior motive, just motive.

He just wanted to experience her. He simply had to. He was drawn towards her and there was no resisting her. He did not want to resist.

"I'm Vincent." That was it. Admittedly, it was not the most charming advance upon a lady but it did not need to be. Never forget how truly beautiful Vincent was and be sure to remember how far such a talent can get a person. "Well hello, Vincent. Have you come here to join me?" She was magnificent. He was completely confused. "I don't really know why I have come here. It's just that I saw you from over there," Vincent turned to point towards where he had been sitting with a now very bewildered looking friend, "and I then just walked over her. I had to." When he finished explaining he simply smiled and shrugged his shoulders.

But a creature sculpted in the form of Vincent did not need to be charming in sound nor in thought as he was charming enough upon the eyes for all the senses. "Well, Vincent, since you're here now and so unsure why that is, why don't I help you. I think you should sit down here with me, that is, only if you want to keep me company. Do you want to keep me company, Vincent?"

She clacked her temptress tongue in her mouth before catching it between her teeth. Which was good, as it stopped her from doing any more damage to poor Vincent's will, momentarily, at least. Then she tilted down her head and up her eyes to look at him through spider legged lashes that lined her lids of beautiful blue eyes. Up close she was even more of an orchestra of the senses. Her smell filled his lungs and was like sugar vapour. "Why yes," said Vincent, "I'd like that very much."

"Delightful," exclaimed his newfound fascination as she softly outstretched an arm to pull a nearby stool out and close to her. She patted the seat to beckon him down and spoke loud so as the barman bent down behind the counter was in earshot.

"So, are you going to buy me a drink, Vincent, or does a girl have to go thirsty?" She was too much for him.

"No. I mean yes, of course." He looked at the barman and said "One drink, please."

She burst into laughter before rolling her eyes at the barman. She then proceeded to order a glass filled with unequal proportions of cranberries and vodka, with ice that she insisted on having. The barman offered a pint in Vincent's direction, to which he agreed. While still laughing she turned to him once more. "You're a little unusual, aren't you?" His eyes darted while he was unsure of what to say. "That's okay," as she leaned in, "I'm a little unusual myself too." And indeed she was. While his exposure had been somewhat limited, even by comparison to the gaggle of girls he had just this very moment walked away from, she was different.

With drinks now before them the silence roared past. She spoke as she sipped. "You're a real quiet type, aren't you? Are you even going to ask me my name?" Before Vincent could speak she playfully cut across him. "It's Fiona."

"Well, it's very nice to meet you, Fiona. Are you here on your own?"

"Don't worry, sweetheart, I don't have a boyfriend and there is fear of me having a husband, that's for sure. Besides, even if I did, one look at you and I'd swallow the ring."

Vincent ran the curve of a smile, as he understood what she meant. This stroking compliment filled him with a sensation that he enjoyed. Yes, Fiona was dangerous. Still enamoured by her, he took deep gulps of his drink without taking his eyes from her face. He was beginning to lose the run of himself. Whether it was from Fiona or the drink was debatable. But the mix was deadly. As with everything, he was a fast learner and before long he used that brain of his to accompany that golden hair with a silver tongue. His efforts became more than charming and he was unlike any man Fiona had ever met. If only she knew.

But apart from his sheer beauty, being different was enough for a girl like her, a girl who craved adventure and the exotic. Like a parrot or some other jungle bird of fantastic colour and splendour of vision, like one of electric feather in a cage, she too lived a life that longed for freedom. At least freedom of circumstance.

It was not long before the girls with whom John sat with had realized that they had lost his golden Adonis friend to the scarlet bar fly. They dwindled around John until he was left to entertain what he could only consider to be a consolation prize. Fiona, in the mean time, was more than enjoying herself.

"Ha! What an answer to give! You can't be from Cork anyway. Where are you from, Vincent?" He paused but was so enjoying himself that he scarcely had any more emotion to be used for panic. Instead he answered as best he could. "I'm from far away, at least I think it's far. But I landed a few months back and have been with John ever since. He's really nice. He's my best friend." She raised her eyebrow and allowed a smirk turn to grin and run riot into a smile.

"What a fantastic answer! I bet you're American." Men entertain women. Women fascinate men. Both are equally likely to fade.

Vincent sat there with a new found feeling of self-satisfaction and a stupid smile on his face. He motioned to speak but Fiona held up her finger in the air before his face to silence him as she grabbed the stem of her glass and finished her drink in a veritable glug of greedy impatience.

She gasped as it ran down her throat and winced and wrinkled about her eyes as her tongue translated the flavours to her brain. With all the confusion, Vincent scarcely had time to react before Fiona reached across the narrow space between them and sank her lips into his mouth. Like two worlds colliding the furnace of his lips met the Atlantic cold of hers and the sensation coursed beyond pleasure for both. Her flavour washed over him, beneath her brittle exterior was a softness that made him feel as powerful as he was. It reduced him to sheer fragility. The perfumed scent that is carried only by virtue of youth flooded his nostrils and made his head dizzy and irresponsible. The invasion of her tongue was welcome as it was foreign and fantastic. It echoed the cries of pleasure inside his mouth. And then, as soon as it had started, it was over. As Fiona pulled away she drew with her all the breath that his great lungs could muster and he was left hanging in poised desperation upon the bar stool. Changed forever.

"See you round, handsome." She softly slapped his face and trailed her hand across his skin as she paid her lasting compliment. With that she was gone and Vincent was taken.

Outside the alley of their flat, John and Vincent echoed their greatness like titans of an arena. Titans, it seems, are very loud, and it was not long before the lights of Mrs O'Flaherty ignited through the glass.

"Ah shit, shit! We woke up the old bitch, she can't, she can't, she can't be seeing you, Vince, shit."

Vincent stumbled as he told John to be quiet before breaking out in euphoric laughter.

"Sshh! Sssh! Stop, Vince, she's going to, to hear you, hear you Vince."

John scrambled about his pockets, his fingers were dancing with his keys, he just couldn't manage to liberate them.

"Ah, no, no! I can't find the keys, I think I must have locked them. I mean lost them, Vincent, I've lost the keys! Quick, we need to head back towards town."

But it was too late, the internals of the front door began to tumble as Mrs O'Flaherty began to open her plywood fortress. John turned to Vincent in a stupour of panic. "She's going to catch us out, you're drunk! What are we going to do?"

***

With that, Vincent threw off his trench coat and grabbed a hold of John. The alley was too narrow to fly clean out. Vincent bent his knees low to the ground and jumped. Still holding John, he sprang clean to the height of the alley, to the point where the walls met the rooftops. There he spread his wings and twisted out over the building and clean out of site. Mrs O'Flaherty opened her door to a quiet alley, unaware of the coat that lay in the shadows.

Flying above the city in the arms of an angel is an event that will sober you in second and John was flying speechless. The autumn air was sharp against his skin and the sound of wings was almost deafening. But this faded into beauty. As John was carried across the sky he thought of nothing from his life. There was no past, there was no pain, no worry of the future. There was only the here and now. They were air bound for only minutes, but the sensation would stay with John until the day he died. It was the closest he would ever bridge the gap between hope and desperation. He was, at least, safe in the ignorant bliss we find only in the naivety of the unknown.

As they danced between the clouds, John's neck creaked and cracked as he looked all about the view below with fresh eyes, hungry for colour. But the greatest of colour was just above his head. Vincent's wings were magnificent against the night time sky. They stole the light from the heavens and were not scorned for their actions. Instead they made the stars jealous as their dove-white brilliance shone with they beauty that exists in something that is powerful and fragile all at once. The tips of his feather shimmered a silver blaze as the beat through the air, like flares to the sea of darkness, the passing ships of meteors and comets.

For all their glory, his wings now made but a whisper as they sailed through the air. John was held only by the underneath of his arms as he dangled above the city. But in that grasp he felt no fear, he was safe with his friend. Vincent too, felt this safety resound to such a different sound. Just as John felt safe in Vincent's company against the dangers of the clouds, Vincent felt the same when he looked down at the streets, so capable of being filled with crowds. He knew John would keep him safe. There were no physical dangers beneath for Vincent, but there are a great many injuries that go beyond the confines of the flesh. Safe in their friendship, John could look up and Vincent could look down and neither no longer had anything to fear. But fear is like water; it flows until it eventually finds a crack. Fear always finds a way in.

In many a sad way, that night was to be their Everest. For the first time since coming to Earth, Vincent felt alive in a way he had never before. His heart had always beaten in his chest, but now he could feel it. He could hear its percussion in his ears; feel its tremor under his ribs. He felt a sensation of belonging and place which he didn't fully appreciate until he had been searching for it. It would excite a want for place in him that he would never be able to satisfy, how could he? So many spend their entire lives waiting to fit in, some are never designed to do so. Vincent was made from this design.

Exceptional as Vincent may have been, he was no less of an exception to the emotions he would learn to be human. For no one fully appreciates the moment for what it is worth. It is only valuable as a memory in time to come. Only then do we realize what fools we were not to savour as we devoured every moment that glimmered with the light of something precious.

But precious fragility echoed in ruin beyond the distant clouds. These storm clouds of the inevitable mocked them from afar. There lay waiting a terrible hush beneath their laughter and amidst the wind. Distant ruin was no less silent, as it was certain.

In Vincent something very different was awakening in his brain. That kiss had split a crack in his innocence. A crack that would soon grow to splinter until it was to shatter. Despite this crack laying deep in his mind, it was no less inevitable than the clouds of the distance. In fact, the two were linked.

Still a little tipsy, Vincent found his way back to the rooftop.

Speechless, John wrestled the access door open and, in his newfound sobriety, found the keys that had been in his pocket all along. As John finally found the words to describe the rush, Vincent had already returned to the topic of the kiss. John put on the kettle as Vincent reenacted the kiss from various angles, holding his hand out like a mannequin. Eventually Vincent sat down on the couch, wide eyed.

"That was amazing, John, I don't know if I will ever get used to this range of emotions. They travel so far so fast. My heart is racing still. Feel it!"

John leaned over and the pounding of the heart against his palm was almost painful.

"Jesus, Vince! Whoa! Calm down, buddy! Ha-ha! You'll be in love if you're not careful."

They talked a while longer. And then something unusual happened. In time, Vincent's heart began to slow as the two men drifted in and out of conversation. And as they drifted further his heart relaxed towards its usual speed. In time John fell asleep. From time to time Vince would mention the kiss, until, for the first time since coming to this earth, Vincent's eyelids closed like shutters slamming to the floor. They crashed outside his eyes and rippled from centre to top. For the first time, Vincent had fallen asleep.

The apartment was like a hovel, but tonight, they slept between its walls as though they were kings.

***

He was late. That was it, no more could be done about it. He was seated on the bus now and it would only carry him so fast. Safe in this knowledge John calmed. There are many downsides to having no life. However, one of the few attributes is that John seldom missed work, and this was his first time arriving late in quite some time.

After excusing his lateness to Tony, the duty manager, he resumed his usual work in the lumberyard.

"Ha, Jesays! Someone had a late night last night!" spoke Bobby, one of the other labour hands.

"Did you leave anything for the fish to drink?"

Despite not befriending any of the staff outside of work, John got on quite well with most of them. There was nothing wrong with John, the place just attracted the same type of people for one reason or another. None of them were the sociable kind.

"I don't know, Bobby." Replied John as he rubbed his eyes with his palms.

"But from the way my head feels, fish don't swim in what I was drinking."

Robert Lynch, or Bobby as he was known around the yard, was the most sociable. He had left school at fourteen and worked as a carpenter, a bad one. He moved as an apprentice to and fro worse and worse grade masters for years. Poor in skill, he was, but disenfranchised he was not. His true skill was getting people to pay upfront, it was half the incentive for his laziness. Eventually he afforded himself a motor. Through a mixture of being cheeky, a workingman and with a set of wheels under his feet Bobby had no trouble with the ladies and that car of his was used to thrill even the most reserved. At age seventeen Bobby crashed his car into a lamp post following a drift and killed his lady passenger. He spent years picking up employment wherever he could. He never got around to the pieces. He was always either talking or singing on site. Even when walking through the evening gates he would whistle a tune. Peace and quiet does not suit men who are not at peace.

The two men continued to talk as they loaded the pallets that Christy would manoeuvre from place to point. Christy was one of the forklift operators. Always pleasant and dutiful in his work, he was a man in his thirties with the hair of a sixteen-year-old, rich and full of life. He was the only one of the yard workers who had a wife and family. He was also the only one who wished he had not. Even though the bars and halls of men he frequented were speculative, however, there was flame to this smoke.

"Don't you girls ever stop talking shite? Where did ya go anyway?"

These words came spilling with a garish disregard for camaraderie and they spilled from the mouth of Damien "The Senator" Power. In a courtyard of loners he was the loneliest and with good reason. A difficult man to work with, this was compensated only by the fact that he was endowed with the strength of an ox. The nickname was as misleading as it was striking. He did not earn it from relations nor certainly not from public duty. It was pertaining to the fact he once beat up a senator of the Oireachtas and received two years in jail for the pleasure. He stood by the claim that it was worth it.

"Ah, just down to the Rockford," said a rather proud John.

"*The Rockford?!* Sure no wonder I didn't see ya in there, I wouldn't be seen dead in a shit hole like that."

The Senator turned to Christy who was stepping off of the forklift and flicked the end of his cigarette away before speaking.

"What about you, Christy boy, did you bump into our friend here last night, or does he not go the *same type* of bars?"

A shrinking violet Christy was not, and just before talk turned to temper, Tony arrived on site.

"What the fuck do ye boys think ye're hired for? Chit chat all ye want but leave the deep conversations for the knitting circles, right? And Damien, pick up that fag butt before I kick yours."

Tony also lived the solitary life, although the others were not entirely sure why. On paper he seemed like he had it all together. At the age of forty-six, he was a good looking man with a good job. He commanded respect from all the men on site and ran a tight ship. In fact, most of the lumberyard employees had never seen or met the owner of the works. Tony ran the place so well that he seldom had reason to visit. But, whatever his reasons, he too was alone. Perhaps the reason all the men worked so closely was their shared solitude and perhaps the reason this was cut short beyond the gates was that not a single one of them was proud of the lives they lived. This was true for nearly all the men in the yard. It is a pity that pride in embarrassment holds a higher importance than wanting friendship and unwanted solitude. But all too often is this the way of men. They are stubborn in their loneliness.

Tony looked at the other three men and nodded his head as The Senator picked up the end of the cigarette.

"Good man, now come on an' give me and Declan a hand getting the next load divided into pallets."

Declan Morrissey, or Decco as he liked to be called was the adventurer of the pack. He was smooth with the ladies and had stories of his own to match and, more importantly, better any situation. A man in his late twenties he had travelled the world in his youth. From Addis Ababa to Seoul, he had ventured all over the Dark Continent and had near misses with bars of modern day pirates in the orient. The southern continent of America was a little less well ventured for him, but he was familiar with the larger destinations. The only reason he was stuck here working with 'this lot' as he referred to them, was that he had run out of money travelling. Since the recessionary times had settled in again, he lost big on all his foreign investments and had to come home.

Yes, Decco had been all around the world and seen it all. Except, he hadn't. None of what Decco said really happened.

When he was seventeen, Declan left for Scotland where he was headed for Edinburgh but ended up in Glasgow. Eventually he saved up enough money and managed to make it to Brittany in France. There he worked in a bar near the ports. It was here that he heard the fanciful stories he relayed to the boys as if they were his own. Some were recited and some embellished.

He was a compulsive liar, and like all liars, he eventually began to believe his own stories, until they became as if they were real. No one ever called him out, and there was many a time when they could have. Times when his stories and dates didn't match up. The truth is that no one had the heart to do it. These tales were all Declan had. When you have nothing else, the men of the yard knew how precious something can be. Even if that something else isn't even real.

"Nah, you're grand, Tony, lad. Let them finish that one, I'm grand to start the next one." spoke Damien after being reminded of his place. But he was not grand, in fact he was far from it. The men were dividing up an order of lumber for one recipient into separate bundles for separate locations. As Damien turned to disassemble the next tower of timber, the stress unwittingly released on one of the supports. In a flash a wall of lumber creaked and moaned as it gave way to the force of its own weight. The strength of an ox, he had, but no ox could hold back this weight. As he struggled against the load he roared for help. Wide hands and flat palms were being crushed against the mass of timber by powerful shoulders, but they only served to slow an inevitable.

Bobby and John rushed to his aid, as did other men in the hard. The trunks began to slow as more and more bodies ran the risk of sacrifice. The tide was finally slowed when the forklift was parked against the load until supports could be refitted. As the men slumped against the wood and slid to the ground with forearms to brows, one man stood, lost in his thoughts. John knew he had to bring Vincent here after hours.

***

Arriving home that evening, John was amazed to see Vincent still groggy on the couch.

"Well, well, well! Isn't it grand for some, huh. The life of Reilly sleeping around the house all day while us fools work!" John joked as he walked over to the couch. But Vincent was not groggy, nor was he merely dozing, he was still fast asleep. John placed his hand on his shoulder and began to rock him. The sponge of the couch flexed as it absorbed the energy, but Vincent did not wake.

"Vince. Vince! VINCENT! Come on, man, wake up! Are you messing like, this isn't funny."

Now with both hands on his shoulders, John tried with all his strength to wake his friend. Vincent moved limp as the couch bounced beneath him.

Just then, Vincent's body rolled from the couch. He hit the floor face first. But he did not fall like a normal person. When he fell his body stayed straight like a sheet of metal and when he hit the floor he stopped sudden as if he were lead in a tank of water. There was a strange sense of inertia about him, as if he weighed the mass of a star without being any heavier than his size. It was as if an unseen force was pulling him to the ground, like there was a magnet beneath the floorboards.

The thought then entered John's mind; what if he were dead? He dropped to the floor like a man obeying all the laws of gravity, down there he listened carefully, straining to hear past the sound of his own heartbeat. Vincent was breathing. He was also still lying face down after rolling off the couch.

John went to lift him back off of the floor. But he couldn't, he was simply unable to move him. Do not misunderstand this, it was not because of Vincent's size, colossal as he was, John still would have been able to at least budge him a few inches if he were he a regular man. But Vincent was far from being regular. It was very unusual indeed.

John curled the fingers of both hands around Vincent's right shoulder and leaned backwards. He pulled with the force of both his strength and his weight. As he neared the extremes of his might, the only thing John moved was his own feet as he glided closer to Vincent across the wooden floor before giving up. It was as if Vincent were a solid sheet of titanium. Flat against the ground, so that not even a wedge could begin to separate floor from friend.

After two more attempts, John resigned to the fact that the only person to move him would be Vincent himself. He proceeded to make a cup of tea and, after the confirmation that he was still breathing; John made dinner and went to bed. By now he was becoming accustomed to weird happenings. When John woke, Vincent still lay as he was. An alloy of Titanium and lead-fast.

Eighty-six. It was a grand total of eighty-six hours that Vincent spent in his first slumber on earth, just over three and a half days. It was four o'clock in the evening on Tuesday when Vincent opened his eyes once more. He peeled himself from the floor and walked straight to the sink. He fumbled, cow-heavy, in search of a glass. Under the tap the pint glass was filled to its brim before it shakily found its way to Vincent's lips. He drank seven pints of water before turning off the tap, a tap that was not running very long at all.

Vincent knew this was strange, he did not usually need water. He didn't even drink the stuff. The only time Vincent ate or drank was for pleasure and it was foodstuffs of great flavour, certainly not pint after pint of bland water. But the water was not holding pride of place in his mind. Having never been to sleep before, Vincent had never experienced a dream. Three and a half days of sleep allows for one hell of a dream, and that was exactly what Vincent had endured. For after the first fleeting moments of sleep, Vincent slipped from the land of dreams into the realm of nightmares. For nearly four days he struggled to awake.

He stood there by the sink, like the guard of a palace for what he thought was only a second. In fact it was hours. Vincent was startled from his waking pose by the sound of the lock in the door; John was home.

"Well if it isn't Lazarus himself! Raised from the dead. Good sleep, buddy? I'll be honest I was starting to get worried there by yesterday when you hadn't stirred."

John patted Vincent on the back with a free hand as the other carried a shopping bag. Vincent did not reply.

"So, have you been up long or what, like?"

Still he stood silent.

"Vince? Vincent!"

Startled he replied, "I am sorry, John. I am up only just two hours. Forgive me, but I am not the better after having that sleep."

Vincent walked back towards the couch before turning to face John. Before he turned he discarded any outward signs of distress and met John with a smile and upbeat voice.

"I guess it is understandable to be somewhat disorientated after such a sleep. You know, I believe some air will do me good. Tell you what, I shall go to the roof and when I come back down you can fill me in on what I have slept through."

"Alrighty, buddy, just don't fall asleep up on the roof..." John smiled and shouted as Vincent walked into the hall "...lord knows I wouldn't be able to lift you back down." Vincent pulled on the trench coat that had been recovered some days before and made way for the roof.

John stood upright again after the new bag of sugar found its home in the lower cabinet. In passing the counter top John saw the pint glass. He never knew Vincent to eat or drink on his own. He was also surprised to see the film of clear liquid at the bottom. He raised the glass and submerged his nose below the dry rim to confirm that it was indeed just water. Puzzled, John held the glass out before him, and then he saw it. Magnified and glittering the light was carried and curved through the glass and into the back of John's head. The light was coming from the floor where Vincent had been sleeping.

The glass was placed back down onto the counter as John kneeled beside the couch. There on the floor were three neat piles of golden dust.

John followed Vincent to the roof, he found him there sitting on the ledge. Both men sat overlooking a grey and misty city. As always, silence was the first to speak. It was joined by the restless, howling wind. It was cold and upset as it violently blew across the roof.

"Vincent. How, how do you feel after that sleep. Like, do you feel well rested? Like do you feel like you've any less energy or do you feel bad or anything?"

"No, John, I feel very well rested, in fact I can't imagine sleeping again anytime soon."

"Then what's the matter, man, there is something not right with you, trust me, I know."

Silence interrupted once more.

The drains dripped and dropped, they had slowed since John had joined Vincent on the roof. The tempo of water flow made it sound like the drains were relaxing, as though they were winding down after a long day's work.

"When I woke I was indeed well rested. But I do not feel rejuvenated in my mind. If anything I am exhausted. I dreamed, John. I dreamed all the days and nights I was asleep and now it has left me tired. Tired in spirit, if such a thing exits to be tired. That is all."

"Hmm, I guess, well I guess I forgot about the fact you've never had a dream before. It's just that... well, I just... "

John did not know how to say it, he did not even know what it was he was trying to say. He stopped to breath and to allow the drains to unwind some more.

"I was just wondering something, something silly Vince. I just...Well, you know the way you have wings and feathers and stuff, well I just wondered if you ever shed feathers, you know, like birds do?"

This question took Vincent's mind completely off topic. His coat expanded as did the wings underneath. Vincent ran his hand inside the collar and felt his feathers.

"No, John. At least not to my knowledge. I have never seen or felt it. And think about it, wouldn't the apartment be full of feathers if I did? No, I have never really thought about it but I guess the answer is no." Vincent looked confidently at John and spoke what he believed to be the truth. "No I do not shed."

This was not the answer John was hoping for. He didn't know why, but this one scared him. He turned to push the matter further.

"Yeah, yeah I thought so, buddy. It's just something that popped into my head, ya know? But then again, I remember that first night when you arrived, I pulled at one of your feathers and it seemed to hurt. I guess they're not meant to come off. So tell me about this dream."

John decided that it was like the evening with the red crystals in the jam jar, it was still not the time nor the night. Vincent did not reply. Instead he simply continued to look out over the city. For the first time he could see the ugliness that John spoke of. The grey and dull and damp and wet. It was not a sight nor sound to behold. In fact, it was not a pleasure for any of the senses. John began to speak.

"Wow, Vince, I never get tired of this view. You know, I know I complain about this city a lot. But I love it. Look at it! I know it's not the Caribbean but, damn, there is beauty in that stone. No matter what I say there is beauty in that stone. So tell me, what was your dream about?"

Vincent lowered his head before raising it back to the view. He took a deep breath in and turned to face John. He looked at him through eyes that were filling with tears.

***

"Okay, right, so I need you to jump us both over the wall, but no flying okay and make it as quiet as you can."

"John, are you very sure this is such a good idea, what if someone sees us?"

It was three in the morning and even Mrs O'Flaherty wouldn't venture to these parts. They were safe.

"Trust me, Vince, we're going to be fine. Now come on, let's jump this bad boy!"

John climbed onto Vincent's back. Through the padding of the feathers he could feel the foldings of the bones of his wings. They flexed as Vincent bowed his knees and stooped his back. The wall was rising twelve feet from the ground, dressed in a crown of barbed wire. In one swoop of dust gathering to replace air, Vincent easily cleared the wall and its armour. On the decent, he outstretched his arms and John felt it as if they approached the ground slower than they should. However, flying lessons was not the nature of the night.

"Okay, we are here. But I will be honest with you, John. I am not entirely comfortable with this idea. I know I have not been hurt since I arrived, but I think you have too great of expectations for my strength. I told you, it is not much more than a man's."

They were in the lumberyard and John wanted to know just how strong this angel was. There were heavier things in the world than those found in the lumberyard, but John had been thinking about this for quite some time. Trying to lift a car was the most obvious Hollywood idea but there were problems with that. For starters, John didn't own one and lifting one on the street wasn't exactly in keeping with their whole low profile agenda. Secondly, even if Vincent was strong enough for a car, he would probably just sheer the metal apart under the car's own weight. But the lumberyard avoided those problems. All the weight was supplied in neat little packages and it was outside the city, no guards, just high walls. It was like their own personal gym.

"Yeah, I know, Vince, but we might as well figure it out for sure. Remember, like I said, you don't lift anything that you can't okay."

A puzzled and sarcastic eyebrow was raised as response.

"You know what I mean, Captain Grammar! What I'm saying is that you know I don't want you to take any chances. You only lift what you're comfortable lifting. Okay, come here, let's start off with something easy."

John led Vincent to a stack of crates.

"Try those, for starters."

Vincent lifted them with ease; he made them look as though they were made from Styrofoam. It was exactly what John wanted to see. He led him next to a loaded pallet of mixed wood, strapped together. He reckoned the whole thing weighed about two hundred and fifty pounds. Vincent nestled his fingers between the wood. With a heave and a lurch he lifted the pallet clean off of the ground, it practically floated before him. John was delighted and began to laugh. He ran about the lumberyard, sizing up machinery and produce alike.

"Here, come over here, buddy. Try these ones."

Vincent repeated the exercise time and time again. Then he called Vincent over to one crate in particular. John had been watching the shipments waiting for just the right time. Today, the waiting ended. A delivery of special order lumber, wood known as *lignum-vitae* meaning wood of life. It is the densest wood on the planet. The pallet required two forklifts and most of the men to manoeuvre it. It was left in the yard because

Tony thought that, even if the walls fell tonight, no one would be able to shift this load in a hurry. It weighed almost six thousand pounds. He wanted Vincent to lift it because it would look just like any other pallet and there would be no hiding his abilities from John.

Vincent outstretched his arms wide and grabbed the cables of the pallet, cables that would slice through the flesh of an ordinary man. John waited anxiously as Vincent manoeuvred himself as though he were struggling with the weight. Vincent leaned forward into the mass of timber, turning his head so that his left cheek was pressed flat against the wood. He began to groan as the veins and tendons fought to escape his neck. Under the pressure he began to release a rasping breath as the pallet shook. It looked as though he had reached his limit. Just then he shed a thunderous roar and wrenched the lumber from the earth as though it were still bound to it by its very roots, entwined in earth and rock. He lifted the pallet free from the ground for five seconds before it came crashing down.

Panting deeply, he turned and smiled at John. John smiled back, but he was not yet satisfied. There was heavier yet, and Vincent was going to lift it. There were no more pallets to lift, at least none that were worthwhile after the last one. Instead, Vincent was led to the far side of the courtyard.

"That!? You wish for me to lift that?"

"Well sure! A guy like you, no problem! You'd lift it in your sleep I'd bet."

Both men stood before Christy's forklift, cold and shimmering between moonlight and puddles.

"I mean it, John, I really must insist. I doubt I will be able to lift that. I struggled with the last weight. How much more does this weigh?"

"Eh, they're about the same."

Vincent's neck creaked as his head slowly turned to face John.

"If they are the same, then why would you have me lift it? I may be from the clouds but do not think me an idiot, John. Now confess, how much more does it weigh?"

"Man, you always go back to talking funny when you're pissed off! All right, fair enough, I'm sorry, you got me. It does weigh more, I don't know how much, but I know it's only a little, a couple of hundred pounds at best."

John did in fact know how much more it weighed, he knew how much more exactly. It weighed three thousand pounds more than the last pallet.

"So go on, give it your best!"

Vincent looked at John in suspicious disbelief before narrowing his eyes and shaking his head. He walked around the fork lift, assessing where best to take a hold. The arms of the lift were fully raised and cleared his head nicely. Finally, he decided it was best to grab the vertical frame of the lift from the front and then tilt backwards, raising the machine towards him in the process. As his massive hands grew around the frame his fingers flexed and relaxed several times before he finally braced his legs. John stepped back, both for view of spectacle and for fear of safety.

Vincent began to lean away from the lift in an effort to separate wheel from concrete. After several failed attempts he moved in closer, this time putting his feet far beneath the front of the machine, so that his shins were pressed against the metal. He took three deep breaths before leaning back with his body. Contracting biceps flexed and strained the very fabric of his coat as though they were about to break free. The machine barely budged. He stepped back from the forklift and bent double, hands on knees. As he stood upright he removed his trench coat. He tossed it to John and refined his position before the lift.

He closed his eyes before one very long, very deep breath. His eyes sprung open as he shot backwards. As he roared, the back of the machine began to vibrate and wobble. All muscles striating and taught like wires of a suspension bridge. As veins began to rise, so too did steam from the October night against the heat of the surface of his skin. As the back tyres began to lift free of their union with concrete, Vincent's wings began to shake and flutter at the tips. Before long they began to unfold and spread wide. John stepped back to avoid the midnight white of sprawling feathers.

But the progress began to wane. The back wheels rose only so high before stopping dead in the air and slowly drifting back towards the ground. As Vincent struggled against the inevitable, his hands began to crush the metal frame of which they grasped. As the metal began to wail and bow towards him he released the machine, which clamoured and bounced to the earth before settling in dust and creaking suspensions. Vincent turned to John, the look of failure worn upon on his face.

"I am sorry, John. I really did not mean to disappoint you."

John handed Vincent his coat as they walked towards the lumber yard wall.

"Ah, no, buddy, are you kidding me? At least now we know you can lift about six thousand pounds! That is crazy! I don't think you get how amazing that is. Wow, imagine if we could, like, get you into the Olympics or something? Besides, you tried so hard with that forklift. And all you can do is your best. Now come on, let's go home."

Both men walked through the yard, Vincent asking John what was the most he could lift, saying that he really thought he was going to budge the forklift in the end, at least for a second. As they walked through the yard John suddenly picked up pace and walked ahead of Vincent. Once he was several paces ahead he turned around to face him as he continued to walk backwards. John extended his palm and slowed Vincent down to a halt.

"You know what, Vincent, you're right, you might be a man from the clouds, but you're no fool. In fact, in fact I think you're not just intelligent, but you're also both clever and cunning."

John smiled the smile of a detective who was about to arrest his man. Vincent, on the other hand, had the usual innocent face of misguided confusion. From his pocket, John revealed an industrial workers blade, the type used for opening boxes and cutting rope. It was razor sharp, it cut the very moonlight that betrayed it.

"In fact, I think you're so clever that you just tried to pull one over on your buddy. Olympics? I think the Oscars are more like it."

"John, I do not know what you are talking about. And I do not know what you are doing with that blade. You know it will not pierce my skin. I just don't understand what it has to do with testing my strength."

John had led them back across the yard in a different direction. They now stood beside a stack of tree trunks, magnitudes greater than the ones that nearly crushed Damien weeks earlier.

"What I think you were doing was pretending to struggle."

"John, I don't understand. What is the matter with you? This is crazy talk!"

John looked to his left, the main supports for the logs were wailing in silence beside him, bulging under the pressure of the weight. Vincent followed his eyes to the ties.

"John, no! I am telling you the truth. I was unable to raise the lift and just as so I cannot lift these logs."

"Ya see, I think I know you well enough by now, Vince, and I'm pretty sure I'm going to call your bluff."

John raised back the arm that wielded the blade.

"JOHN NO! Listen to me, if you cut that support I will not be able to hold back the weight. You'll crush us both. John don't you understand, you're going to kill yourself! I understand you had greater expectations of me but you have to forget that, John, I am not all powerful."

Vincent looked upwards at the wall of wood as drops of water fell from ends of the curves. He looked back at John and met him square in the eye.

"If you cut that rope you are going to crush us. You are going to crush us and you are going to die, John. I cannot hold back that much weight. You've seen all that I can do."

John shrugged his shoulders, grinned at Vincent and lowered his arm before replying;

"Vincent, all you can do is your best."

With that and a flick of his arm John tore through the supports. Other supports snapped under the increased pressure. Before the lumber had time to moan, Vincent spun sideways and spread his hand wide over the load. Only his little finger covered the curve of one row, but it was enough, it was more than enough to hold the entire wall. Just then, the sound of a thud and a bounce shot out over their ears and above their heads. A very top log had gone rogue. As it bounced and rolled its way to the edge both men looked up. John had not anticipated this and was scared. He cowered to the ground, arms above his head in futile protection. As it rolled free of its stationary comrades, the log dropped towards the men.

Vincent pivoted away from the wall of logs, keeping his left hand firmly pressed against it. His right arm shot above his head, fingers sprawled wide like claws. The log landed down to meet the nails of his hand. Each finger plunged and sank beneath the bark and deep into the wood as though it was made from warm butter. His elbow wobbled ever so slightly as the log lost all momentum as it rested, knuckle deep atop his hand.

He looked over his shoulder at John who spoke; "I think you'd better try that forklift again, lad." John grinned at a guilty looking Vincent.

***

The two men made their way along the winding streets of Bandon Road. They were on their way to Powell's Fish & Chip shop, again. Powell's was probably the most famous chipper in the city, it was certainly one of the busiest. Ever since Vincent had developed a taste for food, the boys had been going more and more. However, the novelty of seeing Vincent's euphoric satisfaction from tasty and delicious food was wearing thin at about the same rate as John's wallet. When Vincent had first arrived on Earth there was little to no cost associated with him. But since he had started to enjoy the pleasures of food that had changed. Vincent still did not eat for function, so it was not as though he had to eat three square meals a day. However, despite their friendship and the degree Vincent depended on him, John was ever weary that Vincent would leave in pursuit of a better life. Vincent's naivety meant that he was unaware of how much he was worth. Upsetting and all as it was to admit to himself, John knew his naivety was also what kept him from realising John's worthlessness.

Both men arrived at Powell's where the queue was out the door, as usual. "Ah man, the smell of that food. Christ, we're lucky we don't live any closer as it is. What are ya getting, Vince?"

Vincent paused about the question before his eyes lit up with memory. "The cod."

John's heart sank. "Really? You're going for the cod?" John asked in painful distain. He knew how good the cod was, yes, but he also knew the abhorrent cost of the damn thing.

"Yes, I remember seeing it being packaged in the paper for another customer the last day. It was golden and looked as though it crackled with flavour. It was also nearly the length of my arm. Such a good thing can only be made better by having more, right?" John laughed and slung a hand onto his friends shoulder.

"Ha, you'd think so, wouldn't you, buddy? You've never heard the phrase 'too much of a good thing' then?" Vincent repeated the phrase slowly before turning back to John.

"No I don't suppose I have. It's sounds rather silly."

"Well, it means that, no matter how good something is, you still can have too much of it. That it's not good to have too much of any one thing, you know. Sometimes, Vincent, something being limited makes it all the more worthwhile."

John smiled as he imparted the little wisdom that he had. It felt good. Both men shuffled towards the door in silence. The queue was moving much slower than usual. The cogs were turning wildly in Vincent's brain.

"Well still. I think I would rather have too much of a good thing rather than too much of a bad thing."

"No, buddy, I don't think you get it…" But Vincent retorted before he could finish

"No, John, I do. I understand that *too much* literally means in excess of the right amount. Which is detrimental no matter what direction of the scale you are on. But I just figure that up until you reach that point you can either suffer or enjoy. I for one would rather enjoy."

"Ah, but would you rather not get it *just* right with having just the right amount? Say, for example, tonight, getting a burger that's smaller than the cod but more satisfying overall?" The two men were now at the doorstep. "No, I still think I'll order the cod."

When the two men walked into the shop, the cause of the wait became apparent. Powell's was a spectacle of food ordering. In fact, for the first time customer, it was somewhat intimidating. One of the men behind the counter would shout 'next' and then the customer would hurl their order out across the tiles before everyone else. It was a crash course in public speaking. Vincent would later refer to it as 'the theatre of the poor'. The Powell's staff was renowned for taking vast numbers of orders at once; it was how they kept the conveyor belt out on the street going. But tonight things were not running smoothly. Powell's had been short staffed for some time and tonight there was a new lad behind the counter and he was struggling.

The boy had ginger hair and all the genetic skin that matched. He was pale and his skin looked almost translucent for one could see all the veins that swam towards the surface of his skin. Squinty eyes sat as slits trough his glasses, the lenses of which were fogged up from the condensation in the chipper. He was scrawny and slight in the big white coat that was his uniform.

John looked up at the menu. There it was, gleaming down at him. *Cod Supper: £3.20.* Three pounds and twenty pence?! He just wanted the one, not half the Atlantic stock. It was useless, he could already see Vincent munching away his wages in deep fried fish. Both men called out their order. Vincent always stood out as he always requested his food with the upmost of manners. But the new boy struggled even with their simple orders. John and Vincent spoke of idle things as they inched towards the counter as the never ending queue continued to lash their orders beyond their ears.

But there was a problem. People had begun to return in through the out door of the chipper, their orders were wrong. The young ginger boy looked like he was about to crack and all his worried little insides were going to spill about the counter. The rains had begun to come down outside and people were now complaining from both doors. The manager emerged from the back to see what the problem was. The young ginger boy froze. "What's next?" asked the manager.

"Two bags of… with one battered… no, wait, that was…" The boy was on the verge of tears.

The manager knew that talking to him was useless; he looked around and asked the other staff what was next, but no one really knew. There was chip-induced pandemonium. The manager threw up his hands and exclaimed, "Does anyone know who ordered what?" There was silence from the staff and chip floor alike. But then, over the sound of bubbling oil and the sizzle of burgers, came a voice from the tall, good-looking man in the overcoat.

"The gentleman at the front in the red is having a large garlic chip and cheese and a quarter pounder. The couple behind him is having a dinner box and snack box with one large chips and two cans of cola. The boy behind ordered two Powell meal boxes, tree chips, one garlic, one, mayo and one normal along with a quarter pounder with no pink sauce just tomato and a portion of onion rings. My friend and I ordered a double cheese with chips and the cod supper with two cans of rock shandy. This gentleman behind had requested two battered sausages, a potato pie and a hamburger. The orders behind him were for a garlic chip and cheese, two snackboxes and three cans of orange. The lady standing at the door with wet hair had a dinnerbox and a quarter pounder with two large chips, no salt or vinegar on one, loads of both on the other."

John was as speechless as was the rest of the chipper.

The manager spoke. "Is that right?" Everyone both in front and behind Vincent nodded their heads. The manager smiled as he looked at Vincent. "You want a job, lad?"

"He sure does!" answered John as he looked up and smiled at Vincent, who was now the most bemused in the chip shop.

***

Some things you can avoid for quite some time. Others, you can avoid forever. But there are some things that you cannot escape. There are some things that are created to be inevitable. And whether you delay them or accept that you must welcome them, the unavoidable will eventually find a way.

The greasy chip bags lay torn and pillaged on the floor of the flat, both men filled to the brim. They spoke long about Vincent's new job. John went over the basics of working, but for the most part he knew this conversation was not needed. Especially with Vincent's intelligence and polite manner. However, he could not reiterate enough how important it was to hide his secret from his colleagues. John worried that Vincent may, in time, grow quite friendly with the staff and make the mistake of telling them the truth.

They practiced ordering scenarios and what Vincent was and was not to do in just about every conceivable situation. And then it began to seep into the building. As the conversation began to lull, the inevitable was filling the room. For all the questions John had for Vincent, he stood a naive fool for never once imagining that Vincent had questions for John. As the back and forth trickled to a freeze, the impending conversation broke above their heads, like monsoons in tropical lands.

"John," spoke Vincent. "John. You know you are my best friend, correct?"

John laughed. "Yeah, buddy, sure aren't I your only friend!?"

"Well yes. But I am being sincere. I believe that if I had a number of friends, that you would still be my best friend."

John changed his tone in unison, also to one of sincerity. But it was an embarrassed type of sincerity, as men, especially Irish men, are allowed only to deal in emotions of contempt and jealousy, but not compassion. Still, John fought what was ingrained in him and replied with the truth.

"Ah, thanks, Vince, that's nice to hear."

There was no going back. Vincent continued his train of thought.

"Good, I am glad you think so. I tell you this because I am going to ask you a question. And I believe it is a question that will upset you and make you cross with me."

"Come on, Vince! It's me, you know you can talk to me."

"I mean it, John, I mean you no insult."

John was lying across the couch, he sat upright in somewhat of a jovial manner and looked at Vincent.

"Trust me, I'll be grand. I'm a big boy. Now shoot, what's on your mind, lad?"

"I have wondered for quite some time, why your life is so terrible?"

John lost all sense of playfulness. Instead he was hurt.

"I ask only out of comparison. It just seems to me that your life is very different from most people I encounter, different from what I read about and different from what I see. Most men your age have a wife and a family. This apartment is not a nice place to live. Both above and below have been empty since I came here, and I imagine they have been like that for quite some time before my arrival. I am genuine when I say that you are my best friend. But I also believe that I too am yours."

Vincent could still be quite naive, but somewhere in the reaches of his mind John knew that Vincent understood that he lived a pathetic life, he just chose to ignore it. John believed that the arrival of the man from the clouds really was a way out of that life. Even though Vincent shared the very life John wanted to shed, despite living in the apartment he was ashamed of, John believed that if he never actually spoke of it, if he never drew attention to it, then it would be easier to leave behind. That was no longer an option.

The question posed more than just an awkward reply. It illustrated how distant Vincent was from being human, it was not a question one would ask a friend. Certainly not asked so starkly. There was no malice in his query; Vincent just wanted to understand why John's circumstances were as they were. John knew this, he was not cross, just upset that he had to address reality, something which will always be an inevitability.

"For instance, John, you never speak of a loved one. Have you ever been in love, John?"

John turned to Vincent and remembered a chapter of his life, which he had not shared aloud in a very long time. He played with his watch as he spoke.

"Of course I have, Vincent. Everyone has."

"Really, everyone? Do you suppose that I'll ever be in love, John?"

"Well from the looks of ya, buddy, you won't be short on the women. I'm sure you'll fall for one of them."

"Fall for them?"

"Yeah, it's a turn of phrase."

"How do you turn a phrase?"

"Ha, thank God you're good looking, you know that. It just means that it's a saying. You know, we say 'to fall in love' so that's where it comes from."

Vincent muttered under his breath as he slowly nodded his head.

"How many times, John?"

"How many times what?" John continued about the pages of his paper.

"How many times have you been in love? Is it often?"

John did not look up from his paper; he expelled some air from his nose in lieu of a chuckle.

"Just the once, buddy, just the once."

"Well, where is she then?"

"She's not here, is she?" John raised his eyebrows and looked at Vincent, who was still too naïve to understand how close to the bone some questions can be.

"No, John, she is not. Why is that?"

"Ah, you know the way it is…" – John looked at Vincent and paused – "…maybe you don't. Things just didn't work out. That happens with love sometimes. She wanted different things. I wanted different things. In the end, I had to get rid of her, you know. A man has to go his own way sometimes. So I said goodbye and we parted ways."

"What was her name?"

"Sarah, her name was Sarah."

There was a silence about the room. Some of the silence was for new thoughts some was for old.

"Hmm…" began Vincent. "That is so very unusual. So you don't see her anymore?"

"No, buddy, I haven't for a long time."

"And you don't love her any longer, either?"

The silence returned but John stayed steadfast at his newspaper.

"No, Vince, not anymore."

CHAPTER V

JUDE

The hearts of men are easily corrupted. Their virtues can be the stuff of steal, but so too can they be shattered like pillars of glass. Like a poison in their veins, the debris released from broken hearts flows faster than blood, until it is all consuming. The causes can be few and many, the only importance is that it is caused at all. And whether it be by barrage of force or let in through an unlocked door, once that threshold is crossed, worlds can tumble from mighty shoulders and weak alike. But there can be hope, even if it is false, there is always a chance of hope. And when this is lost, it can be the most corrupting of all.

***

The days began to pass into weeks. Early mornings and late nights, Vincent became a mainstay of the chipper. John supplied Vincent with a large, white hygienic coat. He instructed Vincent to insist on wearing it in order to 'keep up with food standards'. Before long, no one would even question it.

Vincent walked out into the alley on his way to work one day, he was already dressed in his chipper uniform, the white coat and hat had already been well fastened by John. She had been waiting for Vincent, watching for him.

"Mary, mother of God, bless us on this day!"

It was Mrs O'Flaherty, she hobbled from her building and blessed herself in his presence. She closed her eyes and muttered to herself as she tilted her head towards the heavens. Vincent was frozen amidst confusion, he watched her, wide eyed. And then she took a proper look at him, dressed for work.

"Sacred heart! Would ya look at ya, pet! What does that little shite have ya doing?" She clasped her hand tight over her mouth when she realized that she had cursed in front of the angel. Again, her head was back towards the heavens.

"Forgive me father, I know not what I have done." She looked back as Vincent was edging his way to pass by around her.

"Wait! Don't go! I have so much to ask ya! Ah, Jesus, I don't even know where to start and…" again she clasped her mouth and tilted her head.

"No, I mean, well, I can't believe you're here, that you're real. What am I saying, 'course I believe it. I've always believed. But just now that you you're here… what's it like, tell me."

Vincent spoke softly, "What is what like?"

"Heaven?" asked a wide eyed old woman.

"I am sorry, but I don't know what you're talking about, Madam."

"Don't! Don't give me that! I know what ya are. I know your man inside has told you to pretend to people. But not to me, I already know. You don't have to worry about me telling people, I swear. I just want to know. Besides, I've seen ya flying about. At least you used to…"

Vincent was nervous and uncomfortable. He had not told anyone of the wings on his back but neither had anyone asked. Now that it was a direct question, this was the first time that Vincent was going to have to lie. He was very poor at it. She tried him again. "Is it like we've been told? Will I see my Michael again? Is he waiting there for me?"

Vincent stared in silence.

"Maybe, maybe, I'm sorry, maybe I'm asking too much, I just need to… can I see them at least. I mean, you can only tell me what you know but can I at least see your wings. I know you keep them tucked under that big yoke that little shite makes ya wear. Just come in quick and show me, I promise 'til just be between the two of us."

"I'm afraid that – that I'm – that… that I don't know what you are talking about," he repeated as he looked at the ground. "Now if you excuse me, I am going to be late for work and…" The patient Catholic ways of Mrs O'Flaherty were more forgiving in principle than they were in practice. Her eyes narrowed about Vincent as she looked him square in the eye. Her rubbery lips began to contort into a pouted smile.

"Ah, I see how it is. Pay no heed to the auld one across the way is it? Well, I see that little shite has you trained good and proper. I'll get ya though, and I'll get my answers. You wait and see, I'll write to the bishop and to the cannon. I'll tell them about ya, I'll tell them all." Vincent began to back away cautiously, but he could not help listening to her. "And then, when they haul you out of here they'll get the answers from ya, and then we'll all get the answers. I'll find out, ya hear me!"

Vincent turned to leave; "I really must be going, I'll, I'll be late for work."

Mrs O'Flaherty shouted after him, "I'll find out yet, you hear me! I swear to God I will!"

These encounters soon became commonplace routine. Vincent just continued on his way to work. He made friends, he made progress and, above all, he made sure to wear his white work coat.

On one such late night, after what was now many late nights, Vincent walked the winding street of Bandon Road along the short walk home. As the moon mounted the sky, he mounted the sloping hill of Barracks Street towards home. It was here that he encountered the troubles of the shadows for the first time. Perhaps it was rose tinted glasses; perhaps the frames had been emerald all along. Maybe John hid this world from him, as one would a child. Or maybe, just maybe, Vincent was becoming enough of this earth to see it for what it was, or at least what it could be.

"Shut your fucking mouth, you thick bitch. I'm not going to tell you again."

Words were strained through gritted teeth with such force that even the pulp spilled out of the alley and washed the streets dirty.

"Stop it, Denny, please. I'm sorry." Came words that only carried fear and sadness.

For in this dripping alcove was what is romantically called a lover's quarrel. But there was no love here. And as the man continued to coerce the woman they drew attention. It was a particular kind of attention. For most passers by continued in their passing, this was not for them to deal with, it was for them to ignore and feel fleeting guilt. But Vincent heard the voices like a siren in the night and so too was drawn to them like a ship to the rocks. Sirens sink ships.

"Excuse me, miss, but are you okay?"

The creaking muscles budged in the cold air. Both bodies responded as though they had been invisible all along and were suddenly in plain sight. The man towered over the damsel, encasing her in his shadow and concealing her from the street. As he turned to Vincent he revealed her, a fragile woman beneath the horizon of his shoulder. He did not turn completely to face Vincent, only enough to make his point.

"How she is, is none of your fucking business, prick. So walk on."

Naivety is like a plant, if you don't nurture it, it dies. Vincent had not been watered for some time.

"I'm sorry, but it just doesn't seem to me that she is okay and I feel like it is my responsibility to..."

"Your responsibility is to mind your own business and walk the fuck on before I get really cross."

With tensions mounting and the man growing ever more angry, the woman began to plead with the good Samaritan to leave before he made things worse.

"Yeah," croaked a voice broken by tears and fear, "we're grand, we're just talking and..."

"Shut your fucking mouth!" Feeling he was losing control of the situation, the man slapped her with a cupped hand and drove her into the gutter. He turned as he heard footsteps approach him.

"I warned you, buddy, now you're dead!"

But before the man had a chance to strike, he felt the unbalance of being raised from the ground. He screamed as he was raised from the earth. Vincent's hand reached for the scruff of his jumper, but instead, his razor sharp nails sheared past the fabric and his fingers burst through the skin of his chest. Suspended by flesh, the man gargled in pain, Vincent tensed his fingers and began to separate muscle from bone. Vincent's nail scraped the calcium from his ribs. By now the man was shrieking the shriek of the damned. It echoed and hollowed out the streets. Vincent drew him close to his face when he suddenly felt beating at his side.

"Put him down! Put him down you son of a bitch! You're hurting him you fucking spastic!"

The rhetoric came from Juliet as she feared for her wrist wrangling Romeo. Vincent released his grip and the man slumped in a pile on the ground as though Vincent had only dropped his clothes. Turning from the gurgling body, Vincent was face to face with a visage of running make up and bruised tissue. She was beating on his chest. By now she was hysterical.

"God fuck you, you son of a bitch. Why did you hurt him? Why? You're a monster."

A monster.

The words fell like pillars upon his ears. His mind floated up and out of the alley as she continued to beat upon his chest. It was only when she brushed passed him to crouch at her lover's side did he come crashing back into his body.

Cow heavy, Vincent found one foot behind the other as he stumbled backwards out of the alleyway to make what remained of the walk home.

He could not comprehend the feelings that washed over him. He could not understand the moments that had just passed. He clamoured across the night time road. As he mounted the footpath on the other side he held out his palms and began to shake as the orange of the sodium streetlight illuminated the blood on his hands. They glowed a sickly fluorescent orange. As he stared into his palm he could hear the commotion of the alley gaining attention back on the other side of the road. He paid it no heed. Instead, he softly flexed his fingers and watched as the blood, which had already dried on the intense heat of his skin, cracked and caked and fell free from his hands.

His legs began to grind into function once more and he continued for home. But it was not the blood, it was not flesh, it was the words that swirled in his mind. Vincent could not understand what had happened. He was sure that he was helping her. Was she right? Was he a monster?

Fumbling fingers eventually found keys deep in the pockets of a trench coat. The struggle insured that Vincent never noticed the trail he left behind himself. For back in the alley, next to the collapsed couple, and the few spectators that had gathered, was a small pile of golden dust. Just minutes beforehand when Vincent stood in the alley, each time the woman struck his chest and he sunk into disbelief, a feather fell from his wings. And when they made union with the earth they shattered like crystal from a height. All along the walk home fell feathers. By the time he stood beneath the lamp post the feathers were turning to dust before they even reached the footpath. He looked a sight to see, golden beneath the street lamp light.

So too did he leave a trail all along the staircase to the flat. John heard the commotion from his room as Vincent walked. He did not even acknowledge John before collapsing onto the couch and falling fast asleep. It was in this sleep that he returned to his recurring dream.

***

The rain beat down in the lumberyard. The skies of the night time bellowed above. The world was as it was when Vincent first arrived; in restless turmoil. Both men stood across from each other, both men staring each other down.

John shouted over the force of the storm.

"This is your own doing, Vincent! This is not my fault. I never wanted it to come to this! You've left me with no choice."

Silence between both men. By now the rain was torrential, as it soaked through skin and clothes, Vincent replied, rainwater running across his lips.

"It doesn't have to come to this, John. There is another way, I don't understand how we got to be here."

"Bullshit, Vince, and you know it. Do you think I wanted this? Huh? I tried so hard Vincent, harder than I've ever tried before."

The clouds flashed and eruptions followed. The tension mounted in the legs and in the minds of both men. Still, they stood staring, neither one missing a beat. Vincent began to crack and show his nerve. John stood there, like steel in the rain, he was cold and solid.

"Please, John, let's talk about this. This is madness. It's me, John, it's me… it's us… and it doesn't have to be like this."

"It can't be any other way."

With that John ran across the yard towards Vincent. The man from the clouds braced himself, steadfast in his stance, fragile in his mind. Just as John was upon him, he revealed a metal bar from behind his back.

Vincent extended his forearm to block the incoming blow. John swung the bar and swooped it down to meet Vincent's arm with all his force behind it. Vincent expected the bar to bend and slow around his arm, confident in his unearthly abilities. Instead, when the bar made contact it shattered the bones beneath his flesh and Vincent lumbered backwards. As he coupled his injury close to his body he turned just in time to see the steel bar swing for him once more.

This time it made clean contact with his face, cracking his jaw and spewing teeth from their roots. As blood and fragment alike dripped from his lips, Vincent collapsed in a heap into the puddles beneath.

Delirious from this new sensation of pain, he struggled to remain conscious. The cold of the water flooded down his sleeves. But there was no respite to be found. Again the shrill pain of force came crashing down as John continued to beat him, back and bone, black and blue until the bar formed a twisted skew.

The clang echoed out across the yard as an adrenaline exhausted John discarded the bar. He stepped backwards, dizzy from fury. Vincent was pulp.

"How does it feel, huh? Superhero? Where is your god now?"

Vincent slapped out a hand and started to drag himself through the gravel.

"Look at the mighty angel of men! Crawling around down here with the rest of the ants. Pathetic! You, ha-ha, you really thought you were something else. You even had me fooled!"

Vincent continued to crawl though he could barely see where he was going. He didn't know what he was going to do. His ribs were but fragments beneath his skin, his vertebrae chipped and cracked. His insides were swelling with blood.

"Well I've got news for you; you're nothing! Ya hear me, NOTHING!"

John grabbed the wounded angel of men by the ankles and dragged him back towards him, Vincent roared in pain as his injuries vibrated across the stone. John crouched over him, gripped him by his coat and began to raise him up. He then flipped him and let him fall onto his back. Now he was just embarrassing him. The pain was now excruciating and as Vincent lay on his broken back his lungs struggled to fill his body with air. Slowly suffocating, Vincent looked up through the rain, he could not see John. Instead he heard the sound of the bar rattling off of the grit. The black and silver drops fell onto his eyes. The sky lit up once more with a flash from above, revealing John above him once more, metal bar in hand.

"Like I said, Vince, it can't be any other way."

He swung the bar down.

One. Last. Time.

***

Eventually John managed to wake Vincent. Groggy, he turned on his side and gradually sat upright on the couch. John was still looking at his hands.

"Buddy, what happened tonight?"

"I had the dream again, John. I had the dream again."

Vincent spoke in a rush, frightened in the guilt that he felt. He spoke quickly, for some strange reason, he felt as though it were imminent that John would find out about the dream and that Vincent would be guilty of keeping such a terrible thought secret.

"I'm sorry, John, I'm sorry. I don't know why I keep dreaming that, I really don't."

John had neither time, patience nor concern for dreams. Instead he needed answers to accompany Vincent's blood stained hands. He cut across the broken record of apologies.

"Vince! Vincent! I don't care, I don't! I just, I, we have more important things to address than dreams. What happened to you, what did you do? You need to tell me."

Some time later John was relieved. He didn't think anything would come of the man in the alley. Luckily it had happened to a seedy member of society in a dark part of the world that people chose not to see.

"But the dream, John, what do we do about the dream?"

It was now nearly three a.m. and John was exhausted.

"Nothing, Vince, we do nothing about the dream. There is nothing to be done, like."

"But it is the *only* dream I have, John, it is all I can dream about. Every time I sleep, I sleep this world and I hate it. Every time I hate it."

With that, John stared off into space and realised something he had simply ignored.

"You know, Vince, that's just it. It's not every now and then, it's all the time. You're sleeping more and more lately. Why is that? The first three months you didn't sleep at all, not once. What's happened?"

A long pause was replaced by an even more awkward answer;

"I got tired, John."

Neither knew what to say, it was almost as if Vincent was admitting to something embarrassing.

"I don't mean to be facetious, John, I am being sincere. Of late I just find that I am tired. I feel good when I sleep and better when I wake. I just wish I didn't dream about us in the lumberyard. It unsettles my bones."

By this stage, Vincent was sleeping for two to four hours every six days or so, and it was only the start of it. John went to settle Vincent's mind.

"Look, buddy, we've been through it, like. Dreams are mental! And everybody knows that what you're dreaming about, isn't what you're *really* dreaming about."

Vincent looked puzzled; "It's not?"

"No of course it's not! Everything in a dream is a metaphor, something stands for something else. Like, sometimes I dream about my teeth falling out, but that doesn't mean my teeth are falling out. It certainly doesn't mean that I secretly want them to fall out."

"It doesn't?"

"No! Of course not! It's something to do with change or some load of shit like that."

Vincent looked away with a sombre face before a smile crept in and lifted his cheeks. This smile left John in the dark. He could not tell if Vincent had been genuinely consoled or if he was simply being clever and was faking the smile in order to make the conversation go away.

Whichever it was, John was ill equipped to deal with such emotions and, in the style of a true Irish man, he changed the subject.

"I guess we'll have to get you your own bed soon enough, you can't very well sleep on this couch every time you feel tired. It can go over there, in the corner. Right, I don't know about you, but I'm hanging for a cup. Go clean yourself up and I'll make us a pot, lad."

As he stood in the bathroom, Vincent leaned on the rim of the sink. It was a disgusting pea green ceramic that matched the revolting tub that was squashed into the room. A lone bulb dangled on a cord hung from the ceiling and buzzed ever so softly above. He sighed and opened his eyes before twisting the plastic handles of the cold tap. The water trickled as the pipe squealed and bulb buzzed.

He rested his hand back in the rim of the sink and closed his eyes once more. He was sad. He also knew he had only a few more moments before John would become suspicious of his time spent in the toilet. He began to run his hands beneath the flow of the water. The dried blood looked brown against the skin of his hands before exploding into colours of rust as it mixed with the water around the drain hole.

Scrubbing, he felt worse and worse, until eventually he was on the brink of tears. That was when he noticed it. He had noticed that he had turned on the cold tap. He noticed because Vincent never experienced the concept of temperature before. The water felt cold against his skin, it was an unpleasant and uncomfortable sensation. Despite being interested on some level, the idea scared him worse than ever, although, he still managed to maintain his willful naivety and ignore what he should have been thinking. He ignored what he did not want to consider. But you can only ignore something so long before it permeates the mind, before flooding inside. He looked at himself in his reflection and in an instant was faced with the frightening thought he wished so badly to ignore. With that he lurched forward and filled the sink with vomit. Colours of green and orange, viscous and liquid. His eyes watered as the drool spilled from his lips. He turned on both taps as he desperately cleaned himself up. John was not to know. He couldn't.

Along with other lessons that bind us to this earth, Vincent was about to learn that not wanting something to be so, was simply not enough to change it.

***

"What really happened to her, John?"

"To who, Vince?"

"To Sarah, you said that you had to get rid of her, but that's all you told me. I understand enough about this place now that I know it's not that simple. It can't be."

There was no escaping it, no matter how much he ignored it.

"You didn't get rid of her, did you?"

John sank his top lip beneath his bottom one and held it tight with his teeth while he slowly shook his head. Then he replied.

"No, I didn't. The truth is she left me. Not for the want of me trying to stop her, either."

"Why did she leave you?"

"I suppose there are a million reasons I could give you, Vincent. But more than anything, I guess because she wasn't happy."

"Why not?"

John released a sigh that took with it all his humility. He spoke clearly and freely about which something he had been denying to himself for all these years.

"She wasn't happy because I didn't make her happy, Vince. That's the problem, buddy, loving somebody doesn't mean they love you."

Vincent's eyes sank and looked at the floor in pensive thought and disappointment. John quickly began again.

"But neither should it, Vince, that's not what love is about. At least, I don't think so. You don't feel the way you do to get anything back in return. You just, you just feel it. If you're lucky, they'll feel it too."

The light air of their philosophical talk was shattered by the realities John continued to speak.

"I think I fooled her, at the start at least. Or maybe she wanted to be fooled. After all, I was, much younger. I guess it was about eight years ago when it all started. Ha, I was doing then what I'm doing now. I really bigged it up for her too, 'materials handler' I told her, as if I had some sort of trade, some sort of skill. As if I was somebody. Anyway, it was enough at the time. She thought I was great and I knew she was fantastic. She was small and blonde and all about her she was dressed in the prettiest of clothes. Sometimes she'd wear this ribbon in her hair, if it was fair outside. I didn't know it at the time, but I'd remember those ribbons for years to come. You don't see it too much, these days; even then like, girls didn't do it so much. But anytime I see a girl with anything fancy at all about her hair, my heart gets going again. Even though I already know deep down that it's not her."

Vincent had never been more interested in anything he had ever seen or heard. He hung on the words from John's mouth like they were rays of light in a pit.

"Was... was it bad, when she left?"

John raised his eyebrows and nodded ever so softly.

"It was sudden. That was the worst part. Even though I knew deep down, it was still sudden. She came here like she always would. I was stood right over there, boiling the kettle and making tea like a moron, not listening to what she was trying to say, not hearing what I was being told. And then she told me she was going away. Then I heard her. Ha, I remember asking her 'how long?' ha, as if she was coming back. She told me for a long time, a very long time. She said she was just tired of waiting, and that she couldn't wait anymore. She leaned in and kissed my cheek, out of obligation more than want, and then she was gone. I followed her, of course. Out to the door, and to the hall, to the top of the stairs. She only walked faster. I followed her down the stairs, calling after her, asking her to wait, to stop, to listen. She disappeared out the end of the alley and into the orange light of the night. I still play that video in my mind, you'd think it would be something you'd want to forget, but in truth, I can't let the last time I saw her go."

"And that was it? Was it the last time you saw her?"

"Sure was."

"Do you know where she is?"

"I met a cousin of hers a few years ago. I knew she moved to London but he said that she ended up somewhere near Liverpool. Some accountant or something she married. She was too free of a girl for an accountant's wife, but there you have it."

Vincent was saddened that there was no more to hear, but he felt like he understood so much more about John. Why he believed so desperately that the arrival of Vincent would change things.

"I'm sorry, John."

"Me too, buddy, me too." There was a slight pause before John raised the tone. "But that's just life, lad, that's just life. There was obviously more to it. She wanted castles and ponies. I just couldn't give her that, no matter how much I wanted to. But don't you worry. Soon we'll figure out how to introduce the world to you and then they'll see! They'll all see! Yes boy!"

John jumped to his feet and went to make the tea.

"You wait and see, you and me Vince, we're going to make it big, I can *feel* it."

Vincent was nearly as fooled as John fooled himself, nearly.

***

Men entertain women. Women fascinate men. Both are equally likely to fade. They most often do and seldom do not.

By now adventure and the want for desire and the desire of wanting something so desperately had become part of Vincent. He had not fallen prey to the usual superficial objects that occupy the day to day mind of the middle classes and elite alike. He did not wish to see his name in lights nor to have the most fashionable clothes. There was, however, one thing that went beyond a want for Vincent. It stirred in him and it was the very meaning of the word desire. For longing passions had a name and was known to him only as Fiona. Since starting work in the chip shop, the concept of leaving the apartment without John had lost all sense of being alien. It was just the excuse he needed, for Vincent began to return to the bar where he had kissed Fiona in an ever childish search for her.

He also began to do something very unusual for Vincent; he had begun to lie. Further more, he enjoyed it. After the first unsuccessful venture or two, John became concerned about his activities. In part his concern lay in the ever present worry that comes with the cost of such a secret as was Vincent's very being and the burden that accompanies it. But that was always there and always was to be. Instead, John's main worry for Vincent was his heart. His body may have been cast from iron but he had his suspicions that Vincent's very nature provided him only a heart of glass. More still, from what John had been relayed in regards to what Fiona had said to the impressionable Vincent, he warned him against a girl of this nature. "Girls like this are bad news, Vince, they're bad for business, like. And she sounds bad for you, that's all I'm saying."

This is where something changed. Vincent did not accept the words of his friend, he did not heed his guidance as he would have done in the past. Furthermore, he knew John would not like this revelation and so this is when he began to lie. He felt he had to. Vincent also did not enjoy being told what to do or how to think in respect of Fiona. What did John know of her, or any woman for that matter. Instead he allowed John's advice to wash over him as he wore a deceitful mask, one that would throw his friend off of his true intentions.

It was not long before the barman would notice Vincent come and go, awkwardly without a drink each time. He desperately watched the slightest movements of the door.

"Lad, who are you waiting for?"

"Someone I met here once, but I know very little about her. So I am hoping she will return."

"Do you know her name?"

"Only her first; Fiona. I know nothing of her surname or really anything much else of her." Vincent paused and looked into the distance. "Except only that she is pale skined and very beautiful. Her hair is dark and she is fascinating and my friend tells me that she is dangerous and no good for me or for anyone."

With this the barman began to laugh as he pulled the head of another pint.

"Well, with that description I am almost certain I know who you are looking for."

Vincent illuminated with the light that comes only from hope. The barman enjoyed the power of suspense, the simple pleasure that comes from being in the know.

"Fiona O'Connor is her name. She comes in here after work, or sometimes before, depending 'course. Sits over there on her own." He gestured with his head to where she had kissed Vincent. "Mind you, lad, she doesn't sit on her own very long. Bar flies to a spider."

Vincent squinted and then disregarded both the comment and the thought.

"Fiona O'Connor. Tell me, where can I find her."

"Well she works in 'The Upstairs' so that'd be a good place to start."

Vincent looked around, desperately in search of a staircase.

"How do I get up stairs?" The bar man laughed once more. "Ha, no, 'The Upstairs", you know the night club over on Liberty Street, near the courthouse. It's a Friday so she's probably there now."

Vincent rose to his feet as though he were lighter on air than the average man. He thanked the barman over his shoulder as he made way for the exit. Just as he was about to pass through the door, the man called after him. "Hey, buddy, you're friend is right. She's bad news." Vincent stopped only to narrow his brow and resist pushing the door clean from it's hinges. Indeed he could have pushed the front facade from the very building.

There was something alive in him as he left that bar. A passion of flames that should have been bottled up and corked by the Gods in glass of diamonds and mythical alloys. To be used as fuel for stars and dying planets. But there were no Gods. There was not a single mountain that could seperate him from his end. No ocean on Earth that could swallow up the vast intent that coursed through his veins and flowed free to his bones. He had become an unstopable force, an immovable object. He embodied all the passions that every man on earth has ever felt in his romantic destiny. And he was headed straight for ruin.

The cheap lights of 'The Upstairs' whizzed with neon electrons that shared the explosive potential that spilled as confident volatility from the man in the trench coat. He looked up at the light adorned entrance and smiled with elation and the intoxication tasted only by those who feast on wild desire. The girl who took his four pounds at the top of the stairs practically threw herself at his feet. Beauty such as his in a place such as this causes hysteria. There can be no exaggeration nor excess of strain when communicating the splendour of Vincent's appearance.

He posessed a strange iradescence which held an appeal for all. But it was not that of a handsome man, rather the burning incandesence of a beautiful one. Soft and comforting, one that instantly forces women to release all barriers of mistrust and allow themselves to be swept instead by hysteria. In the hue of his flame even the most confident of women were moths to his magnetism. But Vincent was ignorantly subtle about the girls' advances. He wanted only for one thing from her; the confirmation that Fiona was here. A deflated confirmation was all he needed and indeed all he allowed himself to hear.

The club was vulgar to all manner of the senses. The music to the ears. The decor to the eyes. The floor to the nose. And the people offended each of the above with individual and personal discord. It was not long before she appeared like a siren on the rocks between the haze of inebriated sheep. His eyes fixed on her and drew hers to look back at him from nowhere, as though she had been called out from the dark, silent across the cloud of musical debris. She had thought in her memory that she had exaggerated his stunning beauty. She knew now that it was almost unbelieveable were she not looking upon him as she thought it. He could taste her as though she were lightning in the air. She was all consuming and all he wished to consume. The breath of his shoulders parted those who filled the space between them like red seas of fairytales. Fiona started to engage him in her usual playful, controlling charm. However this Vincent was different from the timid creature that she had been responsible for instilling life some weeks before. This Vincent had been corrupted by the power of want. There was, however, very much more corruption to be had.

Fiona was used to having power in these situations, she had been ever since she developed into a young woman. It was not long before she realised that she could get mostly any man to do or behave mostly any way. She had a sexual magnetism that gave the allure of the precious, as opposed to another type of woman who hold similar charms, but whom hold allure in the form of being dispensible. Some have a magnetism that makes a man want them once and, once satisfied, never wish to deal with them again. These types of women are the blatant flirts who promise pleasure like prospectors, but seldom deliver. Instead they hollow out a man until he has not a gram of desperation left. Then, when he is nearly spent of patience and sanity, she relents. And loses them in their gains forever, by which time she has already moved on. These women can be spotted very easily and operate in the absense of other female friends. But Fiona found her charms in another way.

The type of pull that Fiona had on a man was of the insatiable variety. Even if he was lucky enough to have a taste of a mouthful, it was never enough with Fiona. She was like a drug, even after being scorned and turned away, men could only instantly forgive her when she showed them the slightest attention. A soft touch to the face, the grasp of an arm, even just seeing her in the pale flesh once more was enough. No, a girl such as Fiona was different, she never promised a thing, but drove you wild to believe that she had promised you it all. It is a dangerous power to have over man. Power over men is something most women can yield at any time if they so wish. It does, however, have transient effects and begin to wane at some point for most women. But for some, such as Fiona, it lasts much longer. She never set out designly to wield such control. Men would bring these feelings upon themselves. They would do all the work, they would fool themselves. Some times men wish to be led astray. In fact, Fiona was just as much a victim to her virtue as any man she met. But when you are dressed in the skin of a temptress adder, eventually you learn that your instinct is to bite. Eventually you have only two choices that are mutually exclusive; either hate yourself for what you are or learn to enjoy the pleasures that come from biting. Fiona was used to the prowess of her attributes for years now and had honed her skills of the flesh. She was entirely used to being in absolute control.

But for once she was completely out of control. Vincent swooped in and warmed the air around her face as such to make her cold skin dance with excitment. It was too late. He saturated her lips. She felt again to him as she did before, each sinew and line of lip as soft and supple as the bumps of rasberries. The small hairs of the fruit tickled as they burst to release the pleasures that were uniquely human and led to virtues enjoyed by actions reminiscent of animals. There was no priority of words, for breath held the presidence. When he released her, after some unknown length of time, she took the opportunity to flood her lungs to replace the very air he had stolen from her. He looked down at her as her eyes darted before settling deep inside of his. And in that moment they were lost in each other just as they were lost to the forces of temptation. Everything in moderation, including moderation. For too long Vincent had worn the shackles of his divinity. Now he was down with the pigs and it was time to roll around in the dirt. Without need for word nor want of explanation, Fiona took him by the hand and led him across the club. But there was no space for romantacism, no Capulets in pursuit of Montagues. This was for the beasts and those in search of instant gratification. Instead she led him clean past the exit door and inside the women's toilets. The women inside were halted in their condemnation when their eyes fell upon Vincent. Their words of outrage were instead replaced with heavy thoughts of disheartened jealousy. They would all fall silent as no woman would deny or scuttle another's chances with a creature as magnificent as Vincent.

Fiona led him into one of the cubicles. There were no words. There were no thoughts. Just blood that rushed and hearts that lapped in time with expanding and contracting chests. He made sure to hold her hands away from the reaches of his back and secrets that they held. That was the only holding back that would occur between the pair. And there, in a filthy toilet with kisses of adoration, Vincent enjoyed all the flavours that pure and simple self-satisfying sex had to offer. He enjoyed one of the most universal human experiences and was delivered upon to him a new source for gluttony. A new outlet for the ever emerging greed. Just like Fiona, Vincent would soon finish and discover that the act of self satisfaction is one of the least satisfying things on this planet. A sinner was born and delighted to be alive.

***

Just as jealous eyes fell on Fiona inside the women's toilet, eyes of a similar nature had followed Vincent from outside. Fiona attracted a lot of attention herself, more than she could satisfy. Enough is never enough for some men; this is usually the same type of men for whom no usually doesn't mean no. Kieran was one such of these men. Brutish and slugish in nature he had, in place of a head, a rack of pork. Stocky, there was no discernable neck, just a column of mass between his jaw and his chest. He sat slumped on a stool across the expanse of the club, scorned and sour faced as he looked upon the toilet door with a wrinkle in his nose and quiver in his brow. He was jealous. He was enraged and he was dangerous.

Kieran was a child who had never learned that you can't always get what you want. There was never any long drawn out romance between him and Fiona, only the one he had fabricated in his own mind. They had, however, kissed one night. This was an alcohol driven mistake on Fiona's part and the result of determination on Kieran's. If one shovels enough shit on top, eventually something will grow. That one kiss drove Kieran to obsession. He would come to 'The Upstairs' regularly and harrass her with constant advances. Sometimes he would be thrown out, others simply not allowed in. He had learned to balance his interactions and spent the rest of his time watching her and intimidating the men she would speak with. Worse still was the retribution doled out for the men she would show any affection towards. But he had never seen her do anything like this. He wondered what could be so great about this guy in the big coat. What could he possibly have said to her that Kieran had not tried?

He gulped from his pint without moving eyes from the door, he was fixated. Each time that the door swung open and was not Fiona and her new fancy man, he became ever more enraged. Worse still, the hands held to mouths and gasping exclaims of the girls leaving the toilets only further infuriated him. Kieran's mind was driving him wild with the thoughts of what that man was doing to his Fiona. In all reality, he was safer in his speculation than he was in fact, for Fiona was experiencing a pleasure she had never enjoyed before. He began to repeatedly sit upright and fidget on his seat. Initially he had planned to march over there the second that Fiona emerged from the toilet, but Kieran knew that he would only get so far before the bouncers would have him. No, instead he would wait. He would surprise the cloaked stranger outside with help from one of his friends. No one would be there to help on the streets. Unfortunately for Kieran, he was right for once; no one would help.

Eventually Vincent and Fiona emerged from the squalid toilets. She quickly led him aside and away from the door. "Now, I *really* have to get back to work." She paused as she puffed before winking at Vincent and turning on her heels to leave him. "Wait! When can I see you again, I have to see you again." Vincent held out his hands in desperation. He was learning the true depths of greed and the bottomless pit in which it is drawn like a well. "Soon, now go on, get out of here before I lose my job." The smile with which she sealed her words was enough for him to feast upon, for the moment at least. He contemplated staying for the moment but it really was not his scene. Curiosity caused him to walk about a few times before heading for the stairs.

"Is that him, Kieran? Is that the guy who was riding your girl?" An irate Kieran lashed out at his associate.

"She was *not* riding him! She wouldn't, not him. Not Fiona and not in there! All right?!"

"Yeah, sorry, lad, you know what I meant though yeah, I'm just wondering is that him?"

Kieran surveyed and glared as he cast a poisonous eye over Vincent who was none the wiser to his observation. "Yeah, that's the prick who was feeling up my Fiona. Come on, he's headed for the door." He broke like a horse from a stable box and grabbed a bottle from a passing table. Marc, his idle accomplice followed suit.

Vincent filled his lungs with the cold November air. He was very much alive. He was so consumed in his excitement to tell John all about his experience with Fiona that he plain forgot that he simply could not. He had told John that he would give up his search for Fiona, if he told him about this, well then John would know that Vincent had been lying to him. But how could he contain such a secret and such a feeling attached. No, he had to tell John. He would just cover up this lie with another, only to spare John's feelings of course. He would tell John that he had just stumbled upon the club and Fiona inside per chance.

With that his train of thought was interrupted as he felt a brittle sensation at the base of his head. He reached his hand towards it only to have it batted away as he was pushed forward. It took him from his besotted daze and brought him very much back to Earth. In his confusion he turned around to see Kieran standing there, red faced and enraged with the fractured shards of a bottle neck tightly in his grasp.

"How do you like that, ya ponsy prick?!" A few passers by had stopped to watch the spectical – everyone loves a street fight.

"Excuse me?"

"Oh you're excused all right, you tall cunt." It wasn't just Vincent, there was no sense to be found in Kieran's remark. However, it did not stop Marc laughing and jeering in tune. "I'm sorry but I don't understand." Vincent looked at the bottle end and knew what the sensation had been, but he indeed did not know why this stranger had done what he had.

"Oh I'm sure you more than understand, you know *exactly* what you did. But you won't be doing it again, lad, we'll make sure of that."

Vincent narrowed his eyes as he began

"Really, I don't know what... "

The air erupted in shouting

"Fiona! Fiona you dirty prick! How fucking *dare* you put your hands on my girl?" Confused but with more clarity, Vincent asked dumfounded "Is, is Fiona your wife?"

"No, she's not my fucking wife you queer, but she's mine."

With that Vincent fully understood what was happening here. He was no longer freshly off the boat. He could not stop the grin that accompanied his realisation. He also knew that John would not condone this kind of attention and so he set out to resolve the matter as quiclky and calmly as possible.

"I am sorry if I have caused you any upset, but I do not wish to speak with you anymore. So I think that... "

"Fuck what you wish and fuck what you think. I don't give two shits about how you feel, buddy, we're just here to make sure you learn your lesson and keep your god-damn hands off my girl."

But favour was not on Kieran's side. Changes were becoming ever greater and occuring ever faster in Vincent. This bold threat to his new found pleasure and the audacity of this strangers manner set alight a fuse in Vincent. John was one thing, but this creature before him and his one man entourage had no right to tell Vincent what he could and could not do. Especially when it came to Fiona. Thunder erupted from Vincent and quite literally boomed as it bellowed down the street. The passers by had never heard such a noise come from a person before. "Now see here. I do not wish to fight you. But Fiona made her choice in me. Do not dare to threaten me. Trust me, what you want and what you wish to come from this will be entirely opposite to the true outcome." Steam was beginnnig to rise from Vincent, the anger that he felt would have caused his very blood to evaporate had his skin not kept it entrapped and liquid. He loomed over Kieran as loud as he bellowed and the few passers by to become witness to the spectacle knew that he should back down. Marc knew they should leave, even Kieran knew it. But in moments such as this, logic never preveils. It doesn't have the chance to. "Now take your friend and leave me be." Kieran's nose wrinkled and jealous anger was joined by desperation.

"No."

Kieran went to slash Vincent's face with the sharded bottle neck. Vincent intercepted his swing and slapped the glass clean from his hand. It fired across the street like a bullet and evaporated as a cloud of dust against the wall front of a shop. Vincent vibrated with anger and stared down his attacker who was trying to recompose himself. It was no use. As he went to punch Vincent he was again intercepted and Vincent lifted the knee of one of his great legs until his foot was in line with Kieran's chest. His leg sprung out and made clean and flat contact with Kieran's body. He was catapulted down the street. Marc swung his bottle down only to be caught in Vincent's open palm. He closed his fingers and crushed the bottle into shards. Marc was so lost in bemusment that he scarcely saw Vincent's hand come towards him. He slapped Marc across the face and, with the very same hand, embedding the fragments of glass in his face, with some even shearing through his cheek. Marc fell screaming to the floor. Vincent was boiling with rage. By now Kieran had returned to his feet, he did not know yet the extent of his internal injuries. He stumbled towards Vincent. He jutted out his fist with all his weight and momentum behind it. Vincent opened his hand wide and allowed Kieran's punch to meet clean with it. But he did not move. His fingers closed tight around the fist, Kieran's hand was now in a vice. Kieran lurched forward as Vincent kept his hand in mid air, the jolting shock forced his shoulder clean out of his sockett. He buckled in pain and tried to fall to the ground but Vincent would not relent. The steam rose into the ever turning winter air. Kieran was shrieking, but not from his shoulder injuries. His hand was burning.

The intense anger that coursed through Vincent's veins was making his skin almost as hot as it had been on the night he first arrived. He held tighter and tighter about his grip. His fingers began to sink into Kieran's flesh as though it were wax.

Vincent leaned down and brought Kieran to a slumped mess on the ground. Kieran cried and gasped, he roared out for help and pleaded for pity. But there was none to be had. He used his free hand to swat at the ever melting mess of flesh and bone, trying desperately to pry free Vincent's fingers, but that hand only retreated repeatedly as it too was burned. Vincent sank over his head like a storm cloud.

"Now you listen to me." He clenched a little tighter to make sure his audience was captive. Kieran looked through eyes of tears. "Why would Fiona be *your* girl? I can't imagine why she would settle on a weak excuse for a man. What if she were to see you now, crying?" Vincent smirked against the backdrop of Marc's screams as he rolled around on the wet ground, trying to pick the glass from his face and take the fear from his bones. "I warned you to stay away from me. Now I'm *telling* you to stay away from Fiona. She's *my* girl now, do you understand?" Kieran tried to find the air that would allow him to answer. "I asked if you understood?" Vincent crushed the last structures of his hand. Kieran wailed out his answer against the symphony of tears. "Good."

Vincent released his hold and withdrew his hand, with which he took a layer of skin that was like wet tissue in the rain. It stank. Kieran withdrew his hand under his foetal body and sobbed as the few remaining spectators debated what to do. Vincent walked away.

As he made for home he scraped the skin from his hands. He contemplated taking off his coat, for once even he was feeling the heat. But there was something more he felt. It was not remorse, it was not worry and nor was it guilt. The echoes of the word monster faded in his mind. Instead it was replaced with whispers of God. He felt powerful. In fact he revelled in it. He laughed out loud to himself as he enjoyed the endorphin drowned spoils of his victory. He flexed his muscles beneath his coat as he danced his way home. He was impressed with himself. Yes, he would tell John what had happened, quite naturally somewhat edited so as not to worry him. But he would tell him, he would regale him with his victory, how he stood up to the brutish underbelly of the philistinistic underworld. Surely John would be proud.

"What? You did what? How many of them? And why were they fighting you in the first place?"

Vincent chuckled as he thought of the great many facts that John was so desperate to know.

"There were two and I'll get to that in a moment. Don't worry, nothing will come of it, John."

Vincent lept from the arm chair to his feet. "Oh you should have seen me in action, John, it was like something from a novel! I showed them exactly what such uncouth behavior guarantees one and put them in their place."

There was blood still on his hands, black and charred from where it had been cooked and boiled in the street.

"Ah, Vince, come over to the sink will ya, clean up that blood. It's rotten, like. Please tell me you didn't start this?" They both moved to the sink. The blood began to flow under the tap water.

"No, John, of course I didn't. It all started when they hit me here with a glass bottle." Vincent motioned to his neck with his hand and smeared some blood on it in the process. John sighed and raised his hands.

"Ah now you're just making a mess. Here, bend down there so I can wipe off your neck." Vincent stooped as he continued to chatter about his victory. John grabbed some tissue and began to wipe at his neck. But that was when he saw it. Vincent's voice became an echo and faded against the room. The blood on his neck did not exclusivly belong to the stranger. There, where the bottle had struck Vincent off guard, was a very fine cut. Small as though it may have been, it stood out against the backdrop of his perfect skin. John cleared the last of the blood from Vincent's neck. It seems that angels have blood as red as ours. John was terrified. He said but a word to Vincent, who was still lost in his victorious reverie.

The next morning it would be gone, completely healed. John would check again in the morning light to find the skin of Vincent's neck as perfect as it ever was; smooth, continuous, unbroken and golden. Had he made a mistake? Had his eyes decieved him? It was, after all, very late in the night and there had been a great deal of commotion. Why, he himself had witnessed Vincent smear the blood about his neck! But deep down, John knew what he was doing and what he had seen. Instead he was going to hide it away with all the other realities of life that a man would prefer never to have seen. Denial has exponential effects; the longer one succumbs to it, the more potent it becomes, both good and bad. For accepting this, this limitaion in a man he thought without limits, was to accept that there was no light at the end of the tunnel for all their half finished pipe dreams.

No, he had seen nothing because there was nothing to see. Vincent was well and truly down with the pigs now.

CHAPTER VI

LAMENTATIONS

Men do not love themselves. In fact, quite often they hate what they truly are in the present. Instead they adore the very thought of themselves, the thoughts they think they are. If men could see themselves for what they were then there would be no love. At the very best there could only be tolerance. Instead men love the idea of what they could be. They romanticise themselves with notions of daydream and grandeur, imaging lives not lived. The very best frauds have fooled the masses into thinking of them how they wish to be thought. There is only illusion of greatness. If they could see clear and free from rose tint, they would be shocked at the shrivelled creature that would stand in the shadow of the great statue they had erected in their own honour. Men go beyond the love for the thought of themselves. They adore it.

***

The December air was damp and wary of snow. By now vanity had taken a strong hold on Vincent. He was a very different creature to the innocently ignorant vessel of virtue that was once a very beacon of humility. He was fully aware of just how beautiful he was. Eventually, when one is complimented so many times, their head begins to fill until they are saturated with thoughts of their praise. With and without John, Vincent had begun to go out more and more. He could not resist the folly of women. He loved what his powers of appearance did to them. And in turn he loved what they did to him. There are certain gravities that are inescapable and the pull of attention from a woman was one that grabbed Vincent by the waist and got ever tighter. Gratitude is instant just as humility takes a longer time to culture, time that Vincent did not wish to give it. He was now a slave to the mirror. It eventually got to the point where John would catch Vincent in the bathroom in the middle of the night leaning on the sink and admiring his face in the mirror.

He would ask John if he had ever met anyone who looked as handsome as him.

"It's not a weird question, John. I just want to know. Just in the same way that you have never seen a man with wings before, have you ever seen one as perfect in appearance as I?"

John could not believe his ears. "Would you go 'way and listen to yourself. Jesus, God must have had only enough room for looks *or* modesty when he slapped you together." But Vincent did not take this as an insult, instead he smiled as he fashioned it into a compliment.

"Ah yes, so you do agree that I am good looking. Besides, John, modesty is for the misfortunate looking. I have no need for it."

He turned his sickening grin away from John and again returned to the mirror. He smirked as he ran his hand along the shape of his chin. His hair was thick and rich as it was beautiful. "You know John, of all the things I have come to learn here on this questionable rock, discovering that I am lucky enough to come down looking as good as I do, well, that's got to be worth something." John had gone about the business of making dinner and had drifted into his own world; he was far away in the distant mutterings beneath his breath. Vincent pondered; "How do you do it, John?"

"How do I do what?" Vincent dragged himself away from the mirror long enough to poke his head free from the bathroom.

"How do you manage? You know, with the way you are." John stopped his preparation and looked up.

"With the way I am." He rolled his eyes and turned to meet Vincent.

"Oh, I don't know, buddy. I just have to get by, don't I?" replied John sarcastically. Vincent shrugged his shoulders and pouted his lips in agreement. As though he were saying 'well yes, I suppose you do'. He thought John was very mature; he admired how much he accepted his 'disability' as he now saw it. John's patience was running thin. However, there was one thing stopping him from giving out to Vincent; he was right. He *was* a magnificent creature. He was just more magnificent when he was unaware of it. Before long, Vincent had his shirt off; the ritual of self-appreciation was far from over. He would arch and lunge as he admired every sinew of his chest and abdomen, and he would be there for quite some time as there was a great many sinew to explore.

He looked upon his shape like one in a fine gallery, impressed at the work that someone else had done. However it was he himself who enjoyed the spoils and compliments. It was a rather unusual arrangement altogether. His arms truly were massive and packed with the density that allows such strength.

However there was such a great deal to admire that Vincent so easily over looked what there was to question. Gluttony is no friend of Vanity. In fact, he is jealous of him and tries at every turn to dismantle what is lined in good looks. Vincent was eating more and more. More importantly, he was enjoying all the richness of flavour that is found in vast quantities in the foods that should be enjoyed on ration. Sweets and creams fried and layered. Whatever was the unhealthiest was what he desired most. He would joke with John that 'a waist was a terrible thing to mind' but did not foresee the irony in his wit.

There were so many flavours to enjoy in combination. One could scarcely find themselves bored. The limit now was his wages, which he would routinely waste on the spoils of flavour. But they were beginning to take their toll. The definition in his sides was not so defined any longer. Instead there were the beginnings of atrophy upon his muscles. He was still an Adonis among ants, but great structures need great maintenance along with the most divine of designs. The more he had come to enjoy this earth the less restraint he showed. There was nothing that Vincent would deny himself. Why should he? Safe in his ignorance he eventually put his shirt back on. He often remarked to John that he did not know what he found more tempting anymore; the allure of a woman or the debauchery of the stomach.

While Vincent proclaimed not to know which vice was more tempting, the reality was clear. Vincent was fortunate that the kiss of a woman failed to endow the virtue of calories. Vincent used his attributes to enjoy any woman he wanted. It was as though he had the power over women that women possess over men. This was always something that threw a woman off guard. While she would not say it aloud, or even be fully aware of it, she knew that something was wrong. As though the natural order was out of balance. But the extent of his female follies was far from over. He had but a taste and was on the cusp of a feast.

In the corner of the room, beyond the armchair, sat a rather pathetic looking Christmas tree. In fact, it was so poorly looking that it was almost charming, almost. But John was very proud of it indeed. It was the first time in a great many number of years that he bothered to put up a tree, much less recognise the holiday. To make matters worse both men didn't so much decorate it as they did attack it, left wounded and haemorrhaging tinsel and glittery balls. Vincent did not think very much of it, nor did he appreciate its significance to John. But John on the other hand, he enjoyed it immensely and was not bothered by this. He would joke with Vincent that, "At least I'm sharing the flat with *something* that's modest."

To which Vincent would reply, "I'm only delighted that you are not comparing me to that shrub in the corner, John." He was much less polite and altogether more human than before. That meant that he was much more brazen, more direct and in general the negative attributes of a person. It also made Vincent a damn sight more entertaining for John. However, Vincent was not reciprocated in this and as much as he enjoyed John's friendship, he was becoming listless. He was back to the topic of his beauty.

"You are aware, John, that people make a great deal of money from looking good. Men make it from being handsome and women from being beautiful. I've been told that I am both of these things so I should be able to make twice as much, at the very least. What do you think?" Indeed, it had been quite some time since both had thought what was to be done with Vincent. There seemed to be risk at every turn. Despite it being a forgotten conversation topic, John had not forgotten it at all. It was persistently on his mind and had been every day. He knew Vincent was his ticket to a better life. In many ways he already had been. But still, there was money and indeed a better standard of life to be had from all this. He just couldn't risk the dashed hopes that come with loss.

"Well, John, what do you reckon? Who knows, maybe even we could get a better tree next year!" John laughed as he made his way over to the table. He brought two bowls of stew with him. The meat was not the better of cuts but the potatoes and stock were deliciously hot and it would sooth the stomach and mind alike.

He sat and addressed Vincent's comment. "Yes, I suppose that is true. You could be a model for a magazine. But tell me, Vince, what happens when they ask you to remove your shirt? Mm, how long until you have to turn around and show off those turkey tags of yours?"

Vincent, dumbfounded, looked towards the wall. "Ah, yes. I ah, well I guess I hadn't thought of that part."

"No," John sipped his stew, "I suppose you hadn't. Don't worry, lad, we'll think of something in January and it will be a whole new life for us in a whole new year.

"Well, okay then, John, I trust you." The nice thing was that he did. Being drastically less naïve meant many things, but for one it meant that Vincent better understood John's good nature. It wasn't blatant and he wasn't to be named a saint any time soon. But he was his friend and he trusted him. That being true, listless legs are still made to wander. John was to have his work cut out for him if he was to control Vincent as time progressed. "But as much and all as I trust you, John, I still think going tomorrow night is a bad idea."

***

He would often come to the roof at night. Even when it would rain, Vincent would sit among the drops and look up at the clouds. But ever since his skin had begun to cool and it took longer for his clothes to dry, he had stopped this. For now and for some unknown reason, he could feel the cold of the rain, the sting of the water. On the rainy nights, which of late seemed to be mostly every night, Vincent would stand in the roof top doorway, leaning against the wall. He would stand there for hours and smell what he could, whatever was carried in the night time air. But on the nights that the air was dry and filled with a soft breeze, he would sit on the edge of the building and look out over the city. He would hear the distant sounds of broken hearts and the quarrels of the streets, broken homes and dreams that were laid in a similar nature. Here with the poets, the dreamers and drunks, these were the types of people who share the midnight hours. With his palms flat on the roof his fingers would curl the ninety-degree right angle were the roof met the building facade. There he would hold on and tilt his head back to look at the clouds. He would gaze upon the heavens above, if there were such things to gaze upon. He would wonder about his origins. He tried so desperately to remember.

All he could recall was falling. He could remember that it was warm and safe and that, when he really thought about it, he was falling so much longer than the several miles it would take to reach this roof top from even the thinnest air above. He felt like he had been falling for what he now thought to be a matter of time that was closer to decades. In fact, he had no concept of how long it was or could have been. It may have been a hundred years for all he knew. Or it could have been ten minutes. The problem was that he fell from a place that had no time, no concept nor need for it. Of all the things he had learned about since coming to Earth, time was the one that posed him most problems at the start. He simply could not understand the need for it. It was only of late that he felt the true reaches of time. The power of night and day. How long an hour really can be and how there can be so many things that are preciously packed into the lifetime of a second.

He had learned that time truly was a relative entity. Upon first arrival, Vincent had no idea what time was. He tried explaining this to John once, but the concept was so alien that it never escaped from being a passing comment into a conversation. Vincent learned that time was something that all humans were bound to. At first he thought that it was fictional, that it was something they had created, either to save them from insanity or as a by-product of it. The first weeks of his time on earth were as one in his mind. They were neither fast nor slow. There was just fact. But it was only after Vincent began to develop the ability to want and to miss, that time took a hold of him. After first kissing Fiona and the time spent searching for her, he felt the reality in the minutes that passed where he searched in vain. The time spent laughing with John, only to be cut short by John's glance at his watch and retirement for bed in advance of work.

Indeed, after Vincent had begun to sleep, time took its hold over him. The value of a minute when the daytime responsibility of work beckons beyond the bed covers is immense. He realised that time was a very real concept. That the more you had, the more you wanted and the longer you spent without, the heavier the burden of time became. Until eventually, time is all around you, like a newfound gas in the air. One from which there is no escape. Lately the nights were very long. Time is longest for the loneliest.

Over time, his head dropped from the gaze of the heavens and settled on the lights of the horizon instead. There were so many. Some that were constant, of phosphorus and of yellow sodium. Some that buzzed and some that burned. But there was one light in the distance that Vincent was drawn towards. It stood out in the sea of orange hue and called to him in a voice different to all others. It was not a constant light. It flickered on and off, or perhaps there was a tree branch before it that danced in its path and fooled Vincent.

His heart would beat to the rhythm of this distant beacon and he would wonder. Who sat beneath that light? He would look at the light and think that maybe there was a soul as lost as his sitting beneath its glow that they too were looking out across the expanse. He would sit and feel a connection with someone he had never met, with someone who may not have existed at all. But he felt as though they did. He took solace in the thought that there was another desperate soul out there, flashing their beacon of S-O-S. He liked to imagine that if he could see them, that maybe they somehow could see him. He often thought that maybe *they too* were calling out in the dark to be saved. That maybe if he watched for long enough help would come for them. And that when they were saved they would tell their rescuers of the man they saw in the distance, stranded, waiting to be saved also. But help would never come, least not for Vincent. Least not in time. Time, without such a curse there would be no torture. Without such a blessing there would be nothing worth to savour.

In the nights he would not sleep, Vincent would turn away from the view of the city. He would look back towards the sky to see the last of the stars before the dim of the half-blue would steal them away. He would find a star that twinkled in and out of existence beyond the clouds. He couldn't help but think the same thing of that star as he thought of the distant light. How nice it would be to think there was someone watching out over him from either light. This comforted him, no matter how untrue he knew it to be. Vincent could understand for the first time why someone would want to believe in a God. But the more he became of this Earth, the less he understood how someone actually could believe.

***

"As I was saying last night, I still think this is a bad idea," spoke Vincent. The two men walked up the hill as the late December air tried to convince them otherwise.

"Look, Vince, it might not be your cup of tea, but I don't think it's a bad idea. At the very worst it'll be a waste of time.

Besides, I don't know why but I think it's kind of important."
Vincent turned and was almost offended.

"Important? However could it be important, John?"

"Well, maybe not important but... Ah sometimes you just get a feeling, Vince, nothing else. Most of the time it's nothing, but some of the time it's something. So let's just go."

It was the 24th of December and they were on their way to midnight mass on Christmas Eve, an idea that Vincent protested greatly. Like a brazen child, Vincent walked in stubborn silence the rest of the journey. John knew what he was doing but didn't care much. Instead he just lightened the walk with rhetorical comments and mostly just walked with a contented stride.

It had been a long walk by the time they arrived at the gate of the Church of the Way of the Cross.

"John," Vincent began, "you know full well that I don't believe in all this. It's ridiculous fairytales for adults." He lowered his head and raised his brow as if to convince John away from the gate in a final, futile attempt.

"Vincent, I know that. But just keep an open mind, lad. I'm not the biggest believer in all this either, but then again, you did crash land into my life. So for the moment I'm just not sure. You never know, just as you were meant to find me that night perhaps you are meant to be here tonight. Maybe something inside tonight will jog your memory and help."

As they walked in, John dipped the tips of his fingers in the holy water as he entered and blessed himself. Vincent motioned to do the same, but stopped short after John had walked onwards. They had arrived early and the church was nearly empty. There was the token elderly woman who sat towards the front, but not in the very front pew. No, she was careful not to be a 'show-off'. Save for the scarf wrapped around her head, one would be forgiven for confusing her to be a prune at prayer. Or perhaps some other sun dried fruit. A religious date perhaps. But he knew deep down he should not mock.

Vincent had begun to wander through the centre aisle towards the woman who muttered her beliefs beneath her breath and above her beads. How curious Vincent found her to be. There was something mesmerising about her. John had found his way towards the lighted candles and was lost in the solemn glow. Vincent looked back at the woman. Her ignorance infuriated him. She was dressed in a wine coat long since faded of its colour. On her breast she wore a flower and on the other, a pin. They sat like military decorations. The coat was lone and shapeless, with large wooden buttons. It stopped short of her ankles, which were made to look extra thin and frail compared to the width of her coat and the layers beneath. The thin, fragile, boney stalks plunged into shoes that had been built for function, not designed for fashion. They were black and rubbery. Her face was pale and looked as though it had been powdered with age. If age were a white powder than her face had been given a heavy dusting.

Powder filled every crack of her skin. Her lips, however, they still resonated, like a dying candle they were dressed in painted red. Faded though the colour was, it sat in contrast to her face. The sight reminded Vincent of Fiona, of how her lips danced in red and life the first time he cast a gaze upon her. It was the first time he actually recalled something he already realised. This woman was once like Fiona. Fiona, however, much as she did not think it, would once be as this woman is now. John too would wither into age. Would Vincent?

He had always assumed he was safe from mortality without ever giving it much thought. Now, posed with the two options before him – eternal youth or an age-ravaged end – Vincent did not know which terrified him more. He did not like to look at this woman. She forced him to think in ways he did not wish to feel. He turned away from her to fill his head with anything else. He looked upon her with contempt, as though her actions were of consequence to him.

But the contempt he felt towards her was nothing compared to what he felt when his eyes fell upon the gaze of the many statues that adorned the building. Back in the days that the library gave him the satisfaction he now only found in bars, he had read the bible from cover to cover, several versions in fact. He read it along side many religious teachings and found them all to be terrifically entertaining as each seemed to be more ridiculous than the last.

He used to also note how similar they all were. Vincent could never understand why there was so much war and hatred around religions that were all basically the same. But now he recalled them as nothing more than brochures for the desperate. He hated all the characters that were to eternally dwell in the pages. Most of all, he hated the angels. But try as he may, he could not avoid the pull that these effigies of a creature not too different from him had on him. He hated them. Perhaps he felt angered by the fact that angels were so often the messengers of God, that they carried the information from high above to the world beneath. Yet there Vincent was; absolutely clueless to any salient pieces of information about his origins. Worse still, his very being seemed to be without purpose.

He hated the stories where these angels were central to the outcome. He was jealous and he wanted to no longer be alone. But he could not channel these feelings. As is the way with men, when feelings cannot be resolved an anger is born. An anger began to swell inside Vincent.

He looked at the figures trapped both in fiction and stained glass. He was not to deny that they too held a strange incandescent beauty. Vincent could not help but to wonder about these souls captured in glass and stone. Wish as he might to ignore the questions posed before him, he could not but ask them further. The similarities between these creatures and himself were beyond ignoring, even for the most ignorant. He wondered were some of the stories real? They couldn't possibly be, but then where did Vincent come from. He looked over at John who was still by the candles, very obviously out of place and not knowing what he was really doing. But trying his best to do it well. Vincent thought of how they had been thrust together. Perhaps Vincent was not the first to arrive, perhaps he was not the only of his kind. Maybe history was scattered with events not too dissimilar from what unfolded for John and Vincent.

Maybe throughout human history beings such as Vincent have been crash landing into the lives of men and women. Then somewhere along the way, as these confused creatures could not answer the questions of their beginnings, they became meshed and part of mythical stories concocted to otherwise explain what had a perfectly scientific answer. Vincent did not believe in God, almighty or otherwise.

Considering all the evidence he had trawled across back in the days of his intellectual pursuits, how could he. More importantly, it was the *lack* of evidence that bothered him still. How so many could believe so much, based on so little. It was to him a mystery. For if such an entity existed he could only be cruel to leave so many questions unanswered. Such a man is not worth believing in.

The statues and stained glass loomed ever higher above Vincent. They danced around him in a booming chorus of silence. As though they mocked at him with secrets that were common knowledge to them and a source of torture to him. Divine or otherwise, Vincent was troubled much less by what was than he was by what was to be. There was a question that had only just seeped into his mind, but it was to plague him for time to come; if these angels had indeed descended down unto earth, well where are they now and what has become of them? Vincent had never been less sure of his divinity than ever before.

As the crowds began to file through the doors the elderly woman finished her mutterings of worship, raised herself to her knee and bowed at the man who hung arms wide before her. She then hobbled out of the row and proceeded to find a new place towards the back of the church.

In this newfound revelation of question, Vincent had turned to stone where he stood. Vacant and hollow inside he was oblivious to John's attempts to beckon him from across the room. John intermingled with the incoming crowd and flowed over to Vincent.

"Come on, buddy, let's get a seat by the back, you know just in case it goes on too long. It'll be easier to slip out the back."

The pearl dead eyes of marble and paint followed Vincent every step he took towards the back. They knew what he was thinking. They sat on the edge of the back most pews. "Jesus, we'll have to enquire about renting a room here, buddy," said John as he rubbed his hands together. "It's fecking lovely and warm in here! And the size of the place."

Vincent did not answer, he was lost in the depth of further realisation.

The sea of chatter descended into a collective hush as the priest made entrance into the room and towards the alter. The room stood to attention, Vincent, lost in his thoughts, lagged behind in his motions. As the mass continued, so too did Vincent continue to lag. He was not in the room, not remotely. John muttered gibberish through the prayers and response, a strange guilt imposed on him by those around made him feel like he had to. He was completely unaware of the turmoil that boiled in the head of his friend. The priest continued; "and rest onto ye, eternal life in heaven. Lord God, the heavenly Father above, with all the angels and…"

"Enough!" The walls rocked and the windows rattled as Vincent towered to his feet and boomed from his lungs. The silence that followed was the deepest that John had ever heard. Vincent swayed as he stumbled into the aisle. "What is wrong with you all?" The congregation was still beyond the realm of being dumbfounded to react. Never had such a thing been said. Never had such a thing been seen, for never had such a thing been done.

"It is all *lies!* The whole lot of it! But you, you sit there with jelly eyes like cows to the slaughter. You can't get enough, can you? But not me, I won't. I *refuse.*" Faith is a potent fire. A man broke free from the heard just as the priest spoke into the microphone, "Get that monstrous man, out of my church and see that…" the priest was silenced by horror as he swallowed his words and scarcely managed not to do the same with his tongue. The man who approached Vincent went to restrain him. "No!" Vincent threw out his hand and the man was sent to the floor, sliding along the marble almost to reach the alter. No one else would dare, no one but John.

"Vincent! What are you doing? For God's sake… " The thunder of words broke free once more.

"For God's sake? For *his* sake? What does he care of me? Nothing! Nothing! Which is twice as much as he cares for you lot! Fools to the stories and frauds to the teachings. Well not me, I refuse to believe in such madness. A man is not meant to feel like this inside. He should be free from these thoughts, not bound by them. Leave this place and live instead as you yearn. Never come back. Can't you see what they've done to us?" His eyes were now dressed in tears. He looked at the old woman in the red coat and pleaded as though he spoke just to her. He repeated softly, "Can't you see?"

Vincent turned and ran from the church. Both of the large, wooden double doors were closed before him. He ran at them with arms outstretched and crashed through them, the top hinges of one could not respond in time to his force and it burst from the stone. The door creaked as it swung and moaned on its remaining hinges. He ran past the splintered fragments of wood that lay strewn by the entrance. A column of cold air rushed to meet the centre of the church as the back doors stood cold and open. John was now running across the car park, Vincent was far in the distance. All about the wind was dressed in golden dust as the bells rang out above.

***

By now the vanity had reached all proportions. Vincent felt so much for himself that there was scarcely any concern left remaining for anyone else, including John. He was well and truly in love with himself, and had begun to imagine fanciful ideas about his coming to Earth. He was growing restless under John's supervision, in fact he had been for quite some time. It was only now that he was beginning to acknowledge it. The danger is that when one selfishly uses all the love they possess on themselves, all that remains for others is hate.

Vincent would imagine the masses hailing him as a saviour on Earth, how they would fall at his feet. Women would swoon at the very thought of him. Being delicate and beautiful creatures they could be swayed by logic. They would be easy. But the men would be of concern. While they would worship him for the most part, there are always kings who feel threats upon their throne. These brutish creatures would know only brute force. But what could they do? They could bring him no harm. He would crush any opposition with his unearthly power. Armies would fall and in the wake of this destruction there would only be awe struck into the hearts of those who watched. He would be sure of that, no fear, only worship. But instead, he was there. In that flat, in that part of the world, wasting away. He now spent most of his waking hours, when he was not doling out chips, thinking of the life he could be living. He just had to do it right. Vincent was still extraordinarily clever. He understood that such things could very easily be mishandled. He had to get it right. For now he began to plan, some would call it plotting.

It was a curious turn that had occurred in Vincent when he ran from the church. There was an awakening inside him with the realisations that he felt. There was a physical manifestation of these changes that could be seen only to the careful eye, but they were there. There were lines in his skin where there had been none before, the pristine glass blue of his eyes no longer shone as pure as they once had. They were subtle indeed and neither John nor the angel himself would notice them for some time. But in time they would become the canvas of his very corruption. Vincent stood as he always did now, peering into the mirror that he had bought for the sitting room, when John returned from the shops.

"Man, it is freezing out there! Christ, stick on that kettle there, Vince."

Vincent heeded nothing to John's request and continued to prune his reflection. John walked into the bedroom and took off his shoes.

"Ah feck, these shoes are bloody useless. My feet are soaked! Vince, go on and click on the kettle will ya while I change my socks before I lose my feet!"

Vincent sighed like a melodramatic teenager. He dragged himself away from his gaze and filled a kettle full of water, splashing and making a mess with limp limbs all the while. He slumped his elbows down on the counter next to the measly shopping that John had returned with. But as he rested his chin on his hand he was a thousand miles away.

"So, what did ya get up to while I was away?"

"Not much, I must be honest, John, not much."

"Ah well, that's all right, we'll need all our energy for tonight anyway. Man, I can't remember the last time I was out for new years!" John slapped his hands together and rubbed them quickly. He was genuinely excited.

"What time are you going to Powell's, buddy?"

"Three…" Vincent began listlessly, "…or maybe it's four."

John was confused and lost some of his boisterous manner. He leaned in the doorframe of his room and spoke with some concern.

"Because it's half two now." Vincent did not move a hair. "Well, which is it then, Vince, three or four?"

"Three! I don't know, I can't remember what Derek said." Vincent snapped back at John and wrinkled all about his face as he did. He sensed that John would have something to say about this and so began first.

"It doesn't matter anyway, if I'm late all he will do is scold me for a minute or so. He won't fire me, he can't. Anyone else that would be willing to do that job is too stupid to do it as well as me. So I'm fine. Look, I'll just go now, I could do with getting outside anyway, I'm cramped in here."

Vincent turned round from the mirror to see a weak and meek looking John staring back at him. Then Vincent felt it, he was aware of just how horrible he was being. How unfairly he was treating John. It was as if his reflection did terrible things to him. Conceited in himself, when he looked only upon the pleasures and delights of his own face, he could not see the upset he caused in others. The memory of past favours fell upon him and he spoke softly to John.

"And besides, you're right, I had best get there for three, hadn't I? You know when I was too silly to listen. I should be done at eleven or there abouts and then we'll go to town." He smiled softly at John.

"Sounds good, Vince, where'll we go?"

"Anywhere you want, my friend."

"Just not The Upstairs, right?"

Vincent smiled, "Right, anywhere but there. I'll see you tonight."

Vincent dressed for work and left the apartment. John was left with only the vapour of his breath in the air. He unpacked the shopping and, as always, sat down with his newspaper. He settled underneath the blankets of the couch and it was not long before he dozed off.

When he awoke he was all in darkness. He was cold and disorientated. There was only the sliver of orange light that broke free from his bedroom window through the open door of his room. He fumbled in the dark to find the wall switch. The low intensity of the light still hurt his eyes. He looked at the clock; it was eleven twenty-five. Vincent would be home any minute and John was only just awake. He ran to the bathroom and pulled his shirt from his body. He ran the hot tap despite knowing that it would do no good, there would only be cold water for him to use. He splashed handful after handful under his arms, half wanting it on his skin while half dodging it.

He rubbed vigorously, to keep warm more than to actually clean. He grabbed the towel from the pea green bathtub, it was already wet and cold with damp. It moved the water around his arms more than it dried them. He ran back to the sitting room and looked at the clock; eleven thirty-five. Vincent was still not home. This was very unusual, he was never late back from Powell's. It was, at best, an eight-minute walk and it was downhill all the way home. John decided to start walking towards the chipper, that way he would meet Vincent along the way.

The streets were quiet, it would be new years' in fifteen minutes and everyone was already in town. John rounded the bend to where the street turned into a straight line all the way down to the chipper. There was no sign of Vincent walking towards him. He reached Powell's where all the lights were turned off, there was just the glow from a backroom light far beyond the counter. John knocked on the glass of the door. He knocked for some time, getting harder and louder. He heard muffled shouts from the back, through the glass he could scarcely make out the words. Derek walked through the dimly lit shop front, cursing as he made his way to the door, "For fuck sake, I said we're closed! Now feck off and get chips somewhere else, I'm going home for…" he opened the door and was surprised to see John standing there in the cold.

"Ah, John! Sorry, lad, I didn't know it was yourself." He was still somewhat agitated, "what are you doing here?"

"I'm sorry to be at ya, Derek, I just came by to get Vince, ye must have been busy to keep him this late!" The nervous laughter made the situation all the more awkward. Derek scratched the back of his head and looked down at the floor.

"Ah, John, lad. Vince isn't here."

"He's not?"

"No, he's not. He went to town with two of the boys, almost an hour ago." Derek was embarrassed for John as he knew what had happened. He offered him a bag of chips but John politely refused as he tried to cover up what had happened.

"Oh yes, you're right! Feck yeah, I remember now, I was meant to be meeting them in town. I fell asleep and I guess, I guess I got confused and I forgot…"

"Anyway, John, look I'd better lock up, it's late. Happy New Year to ya."

"Yeah, yeah of course, happy New Year."

John turned to walk away when Derek called after him. "Do you know where they went?" Still walking, John said back, "I know exactly where he's gone."

John thought that maybe he had misheard Vincent, that maybe they were meant to meet in town. But these thoughts were just self-comforting lies of denial. He knew very well that Vincent had ditched him. He also knew he should just go home, that no good would come from storming in where he was not wanted. But it was no use. John made way for town. His anger swelled until it was replaced with sheer heartache; just as he neared town he heard the church bells and sounds of the city usher in the New Year. John stood there, in the cold of the street, all alone for yet another year. But this was worse than all the other years, for this time he had gotten his hopes up. This year the disappointment was sharper than ever and cut far beneath the skin. The moment passed and when it did he was even more enraged with Vincent than when he left from Powell's.

He continued down Bishops Street and made his way over Wandesford Quay Bridge. John was headed straight for where he knew Vincent would be, he was headed for The Upstairs.

As he walked through the front door the bouncer's joked "Aren't you a little late there, pal?" John paid them no attention. Their laughter only served to fuel his rage.

He arrived upstairs to a room of inebriation. The passionate kisses that ushered in New Years had either died out or had grown. It would not be difficult to find Vincent, he was undoubtedly with some new flavour of the night. John's thoughts mocked and condemned in jealous rage. The fool, all the powers he had been sent to earth with and *this* is how he uses them. As expected, he found Vincent sat on one of the dim-lit couches. He was running his fingers through the dark hair of a Fiona look-a-like as he whispered charming lies into her ear between kisses of her neck. The girl giggled and reeled at his every word. She trembled and lusted for every kiss. Vincent saw John marching towards him but pretended he did not. He continued on hoping that John would simply walk away.

John reached down and slapped Vincent's hand from her neck. He pushed him away from the girl.

"What's your problem!" exclaimed the girl. But John did not respond. He only looked at Vincent who would not yet look at him. Not needing any trouble to be her own, the girl picked up her drink and walked away carefree. At that point Vincent jumped to his feet.

"John! My friend, you made it finally! I was worried you weren't coming."

"Don't give me that shit you son of a bitch. You ditched me, you came here without me on purpose. Why, Vincent, why did you do this?"

Vincent grabbed his pint glass and squinted his face as if he had no idea what John was talking about.

"Why did I do what, John, I thought we were meeting here. Remember, you said The Upstairs today in the apartment?" John knew what he was doing.

"No I didn't, Vincent, and neither did you." Vincent no longer cared about being convincing, as he looked at passersby instead of John he answered nonchalantly, "Oh really, sorry I could have been more than certain we did…" As he trailed off John's anger was converted to upset. His friend had let him down.

"Why, Vince, why didn't you want me to come out with you?"

The angel, although having done a horrible thing, had not yet dealt with awkward feelings of guilt such as this. He did not know where to look nor what to say.

"I don't know, John, I guess that I was confused. I made a mistake and I am sorry. It won't happen again. But look, you're here now so we should make the most of it and enjoy ourselves, yes?"

After finding Vincent and saying what he wanted to say, John had little more to do and he didn't have a plan beyond this point. But most of all, he just wanted these feelings to go away. He would have agreed to Satan himself if it relieved him of this moment. Vincent put his hand on his friend's shoulder and looked him in the eye; "John?"

"Yeah, I suppose you're right. I guess we should just try and have some fun."

Vincent was equally relieved of the situation.

"That's the spirit! Why don't you wait here and start enjoying the music while I get us some drinks, yes?"

John nodded as Vincent sailed for the bar. He was hollow inside.

As he began to calm, a wave of embarrassment began to wash over John. He wore the shame of his feelings like a coat of terrible colours, bright for all to see and none to hide from. He thought that perhaps it was childish, the way he acted. What right had he to speak to Vincent like that? That girl, oh the embarrassment he now felt. She must have thought John was crazy. He decided to walk to the bar and buy the first drink. But on his way he discovered that Vincent was having his very own separate thoughts on the other side of the club. There he stood, no drinks in hand, he hadn't even made it to the bar, he stood talking to another girl, this time blonde.

"I mean it, I have never in all my time seen a creature as magnificent as you."

The girl laughed at the comment, but deep down she enjoyed it and wanted more.

"Will ya stop? Jesus, the shite coming out of ya. Besides, I can't, my fella is meant to be meeting me here soon anyway."

All the charm that Vincent could muster carried his words like chocolate for ears as he replied, "Well, in that case we'd better be quick." He smiled with delight as she led him off towards the dark corners of the club. Just then Vincent felt a strong tug upon his arm.

"What are you doing? Can you not help yourself, like?"

"John don't..."

"I mean it, do you love yourself that much that you need everyone else to love you as well?"

"Just leave me be and go home, John. We'll talk about it another time, I am otherwise engaged at this moment."

John could not believe what had become of Vincent. What had happened to his friend and to their friendship? Indeed, what it meant for all his ill-thought hopes and plans.

"Vince, stop, don't go with her, you can't do this." Vincent turned and snarled at his friend.

"No, John, that's where you're mistaken. *You* can't do this, I can. Now go home."

Vincent walked away with the young lady, shouting whispers into her ear to quickly explain away his friend. John stormed from the club and made his way back home. He was a bag of emotions, all fighting for control, each more desperate than the other. They were all John had.

But he was barely back at Wandesford Quay Bridge when he realized that he had left the flat without his keys. He was locked out. He would have to return to Vincent, tail between his legs and get his keys. His heart could scarcely take another confrontation like the one he just had. He had heard enough truths for one night.

But as he walked down behind the courthouse towards The Upstairs he heard the screams of a young woman. Her frightened voice was calling them to stop. As John neared the nightclub he saw a figure stumbling to the ground as four men attacked him. It was Vincent. The men were kicking and stamping on Vincent, who was dazed and confused on the ground. One man spoke as the others continued.

"Who the fuck do you think you are, huh? Putting your hands all over my girl like that?" The irony of déjà vu was lost on Vincent who struggled to comprehend the situation. He had never been in pain before. It was a terrifying experience. The men continued to kick him as they jeered. Vincent was lost between terror, confusion and pain.

John ran in without thinking and tackled one of them to the ground with the element of surprise. One of the men went to help his friend. He punched John in the back of the head and he fell over. In his anguish he released a shout, to which Vincent turned his head.

He saw John there on the wet ground, looking at him. There was blood all over Vincent's face. The two men met with eyes of solidarity. Then John was kicked relentlessly. It was enough to bring Vincent back. He grabbed the next boot that swung towards his face and twisted it sharply, he split the anklebones clean from the skin. The man screamed out in pain. It was enough for Vincent to get to his feet, he was still clumsy and dazed. But he got up to help John. As the man screamed in pain it was now just the scorned boyfriend who was attacking Vincent.

Vincent punched him in the ribs and the street was alive with the sound of cracked bones. But Vincent grimaced in pain, as the man bent over, Vincent shook his hand in the air, as if the punch had hurt him too. He lunged forward and grabbed the man by the neck and, using his remaining strength, threw him at the men who were still kicking John. He knocked one over and the other man, now sparse and empty of comrades, assessed the situation and ran away. Vincent fell to one knee by John's side. The distance rang out with the sound of sirens. "Vince, Vince, help me up. We gotta get out of here. Now!"

Both men stumbled into their alleyway, they were short on breath from helping each other. They stopped short of the door. They were finally safe now. John leaned against the wall as Vincent slumped. Both were trying to process what had happened and what it meant for them. The men had bottled Vincent as he walked down the stairs of the club. He fell down the flight of stairs and was dazed. That was when they jumped him. His head and neck had been cut pretty badly. But as Vincent was strewn against the wall, now was when the real fear settled into his bones. He felt the fleshy wounds on the back of his head. The pain was much less, but he was numb to the world. What was happening to him? How did he become this way? He was becoming more frightened with each passing second. As with so many, Vincent did something truly human; in a time of great hardship and fear, Vincent took his feelings out on the one person who cared for him most.

"This is all your fault." He muttered against the wall. John, who himself was in agony did not believe what he heard and softly asked "What, Vince?"

"I said this is *your* fault! This is your doing, John!"

"How? How is it my fault, Vince?"

"I would have never been talking to her if you hadn't shown up!"

"Are you mad? Are you completely fucking mental! Are you even going to thank me for rushing to your help? If you don't remember, I was nearly kicked to death back there over you! So don't you start telling me…"

"I mean it, John, it's your fault! It's just, it's just… aahh!"

Vincent threw off his coat and started to run down the alley. He spread his wings and jumped into the sky to fly away. But he only drifted a few feet into the air before falling back down to earth. He dragged his skin as he grated along the gravel. Vincent was no longer able to fly.

He lay there, as his wings softly folded back over his body and began to cry. His wings were frail and there were great patches of feathers missing. The feathers that remained were stained and clogged with blood. They reflected the light of the New Year moon like a gull in an oil spill.

John looked at him, for the first time since Vincent had come into his life, John no longer felt like the weak one.

***

In less than a week into 1985 Vincent's wounds had completely healed. The cuts and gashes on his head had all closed up. His hair sat like a mannequin over where the wounds had been. The bruises on his face and body had all disappeared, there was no discolouration, no evidence that any struggle had occurred at all.

John, on the other hand, would take a much longer time to repair. He was rattled and easily startled for some time. His body showed all the ruin of a man who was struggling to heal. For a week his lips were blistered and tight to the touch, still swollen, much like the rest of his face. His skin was dotted and blotched in an archipelago of sick yellows and deep blue bruises. He did not know it, but two of his ribs had been cracked in the fight. His body took a long time to heal.

Neither man mentioned anything that had happened that night. Both were much happier pretending that reality had not happened. However, there was one question that John simply had to ask. He suddenly raised it with Vincent as they both sat one night in that silent apartment.

"Vince, why did you have to pick her? Why that girl? I mean, you said that you knew she had a boyfriend. You probably could have had any other girl in that place. So why her?"

Vincent smiled to himself, as he knew something John just didn't understand. He sat upright on the sofa to explain.

"Because, the ones with the boyfriends are always more exciting."

"More exciting, how do you make that so?"

"Because they know that it's wrong. And that makes it exciting all the way through. With a single girl, the thrill and excitement starts to fade once she's yours. But when you're with a woman who has promised herself to another, well, it is only when you start to kiss that the passion and excitement kicks in."

John understood what he meant, but he was no less disgusted by it.

"Vince, isn't that kind of wrong, like?"

Vincent laughed and rolled his eyes.

"Wrong? What does that even mean, John? What is wrong; what is right? None of it matters in the end. Besides, if it were not me that those women were with it would be someone else."

The room fell silent. John did not agree with Vincent, but he secretly confessed to himself that if he had Vincent's looks he too would probably do the same. Vincent continued; "You know, they seem from the outside to require more work. That a taken girl is harder to convince. But the truth is, they're easier if anything. They just look like they require more work because you have to spend longer talking to them, but that doesn't mean it takes longer to convince them."

"I don't follow you?"

"Because, John, with a single girl, nearly the whole conversation is built around convincing her. But with a taken girl, well they're practically convinced from the start. The rest of the conversation is just what they want to hear. You see, they're starving for attention. They see the other girls, their friends who are freely approached by man after man, watch them shoot them down because they can, because they have the pick. But taken girls, well they feel like they're gathering dust on the shelf and get so excited at the thought of being bought that they're damn near free."

"And you *like* that?"

"I love it, John. Their eyes come to life when you talk to them. Their blood starts to rush like it used to back when things were exciting. I feel like a God, giving them life again. They make me feel new, John."

Once more, the silence that had become a part of the flat fell between them. They sat for a few moments before Vincent finally added; "But most of all, most of all, they just can't help themselves. And neither can I. But I don't think we'd take the help, even if it was offered to us. Just because I can't help myself, doesn't mean I want someone else to."

But it was Vincent who felt the reaches of the incident on New Year's far more and for far longer than John. For all of his healing, for all of his miraculous repair his wings were still missing feathers. They had not healed like the rest of his body. In fact, they were much worse. He was losing feathers by the day but he was in a state of denial. John would not notice for

221

quite some time because after that night, Vincent always wore his coat around the flat. There was a time when John would come home from work to see Vincent crouched and perched on the end of the sofa with his glorious white wings stretched out across the span of the room, lost in whatever book he was reading. But not anymore.

Now the only sight of Vincent that John was greeted with was Vincent wrapped up, lying on the couch in silence. Over the coming weeks, Vincent became more and more withdrawn. The reaches of the New Year's fight were long as they were lasting. What was more, their effects had started to take their toll. It was not long before those subtle signs of Vincent's change became not so subtle. The signs that were once hard to notice became a struggle to ignore.

The lines on his face began to deepen into wrinkles and were soon joined by more. His hair had lost its vitality. A crown fashioned from full locks of flowing golden hair no longer adorned his head. Instead it was limp and flat. It became greasy and lost its colour. The tint began to fade like an old television losing its technicolour. Furthermore, John would find more and more strands about the flat. Vincent's hair was falling out. His teeth began to stain and show the marks of his gluttony, the same was true of his body. He was ever losing the stone cut definition in his muscles. They became less dense and more plump. There was a roundness to his body as what was ripped soon started to become rippled. His skin began to flake and crack. His nails became chipped and jagged as the skin of his hands grew ever more course. He had lost the softness in his touch.

But what struck John the most were Vincent's eyes. His eyes had lost their glimmer of ice, their passion of fire. They were no longer discs of startling blue that welcome one to look upon them. Before there was an innocence in his eyes, there was something comforting in his gaze. They were eyes that lulled you to become lost in his trance. But now he peered out at the world through cloudy eyes of hazy grey. The loss of the beauty in his eyes only served to accentuate the other changes in Vincent. They were murky and made John feel that he was talking to a different person. He was.

These changes were the physical manifestation of the turmoil that consumed Vincent. He began to rot from the inside out. He was no longer as cocky and confidant as he had once been. Instead he was frail and week. John began to worry as he would hear him coughing in his sleep. Sleep. Vincent slept every single night now and had even began to nap in the evenings, all the while having the same dream over and over again. He began to become exhausted from the dream. However, there was one change. Sometimes, the metal bar in the dream that John used as a weapon was substituted with an old, metal clasped suitcase. He told John this on several occasions but it was further evidence for John to laugh the dream away. Maybe he was right, maybe it meant nothing to Vincent. He no longer woke in a stupor nor a sweat. Instead his eyes would open with a hollow terror, a feeling of unease that he simply could not settle. Vincent also had a thirst, an insatiable thirst that he simply could not satisfy. He would wake to fill glass after glass of water but he could get no relief from his want of the lips. He tried everything, water did nothing, milk would only fill him, alcohol only made him cross and angry but did nothing for his thirst. Sometimes he felt he would die if he did not get an end to his satisfaction.

For the first time he felt all the cold that Irish air had to offer, the damp seemed to saturate his skin and weigh him down. The dark of the evenings settled on his shoulders like the depression of so many of the same shore. But the morning light was no saviour to him, he could see no hopeful horizon, only the harshness of the morning sky. Vincent was well and truly miserable. All around him was a struggle.

***

"John, I'm tired, John."

"Then have a rest, buddy."

"No, John, it does no good. Not anymore. I'm so tired John, I'm so tired all the time. When I wake, it's worse. It's as if I never slept at all. I'm just so tired, John. I want it to stop."

There was nothing but silence between them.

"I don't know what to say, Vincent."

Vincent's eyes glazed over as he looked at the floor, his mouth barely moving as he spoke.

"That's okay, John, because I don't know what I want to hear from you. Does everyone feel like this, eventually?"

Like what?

"Awful."

John began with a comforting laugh.

"Ah, buddy, cheer up, it's not that bad!"

"Really? Is it not, John? Because what am I doing here. I feel hollow, John, I feel like the world has grown cold and is going to continue until I am frozen solid."

John awkwardly started to fold his newspaper.

"I think of her sometimes," spoke Vincent.

"Of, Fiona?"

"No, I think of *her* all the time. Rose."

"Rose?"

"The librarian. Rose. She was nice to me. I scared her, but she was nice to me."

Vincent stopped only to refill his lungs, never to blink. He stayed sprawled with floor fixed, glazed eyes.

"You know, I understand why we stopped talking. I scared her. And that was that. I just gave up on her, without so much as the question of a fight. You know, she liked me, John."

"I bet she did, Vince, all girls seem to like you."

Vincent shuddered through his whole body and squinted his face as though he was in anguish.

"No, John, I mean she really liked me. Not because of how I looked, but because of who I was. Even before I was here long enough to actually be anyone. Back when I was happy to read all day and learn about fabulous things. But she was the fabulous thing. She liked me back when I was good."

"Buddy, would ya stop! You are good! Sure, what's wrong with you?"

Vincent turned his eyes to look at John. They narrowed with contempt.

"You just don't get it, John."

John was hurt. He was about to go on the offensive until Vincent's face softened and his eyes fell back to the floor.

"I don't think I get it either. You know, Fiona had never really wanted much to do with me, she wasn't even that nice. But it's not Rose I go out to bars to find, it's her. What's wrong with me that I think about someone who doesn't even want me more than I think about a nice girl I scared half to death? A girl I scared away. Rose was nice. I think I'd be better if I had seen her more. But still, I think instead for Fiona, just like I see you drifting into the thoughts you have for Sarah."

John tensed up, as if he had just been embarrassed in front of a large room of people. There was nothing to say back to that comment. Sometimes there is no refuting the truth.

There was silence once more.

"I'm sorry, John."

"Sorry for what?"

"I know you thought your life would get better when I arrived, that I was your ticket out of here…"

The lack of a reply from John made the situation more awkward and pathetic than it already was.

"…but how can I save you when I can't even save myself?"

"I'll think of something, Vince. I'll think of something. I know my life is meant to get better. I know it is. You're the answer, Vincent. You and me, together we'll make it good for both of us. You and me, buddy, you and me. I know it sounds stupid but I have a feeling, Vincent, we're going to make it and it will be good. In the end, it'll be you and me."

John was so convincing he almost believed himself. Vincent dragged a smile across his face like lies across gravel and looked at John.

"Yes, you and me."

***

The weeks continued to pass. The men drifted further every day. Silence turns friends into strangers. While Vincent was lost in the depths of facing the ever more apparent realities of what was happening to him, John was still choosing to hold on to denial.

As he worked in the lumberyard he still thought that something could be salvaged. He believed in Vincent, he had to. He had vested so much interest in him for so long that he could not face what was happening. More still, he did not want to come to terms with the fact that the only friend he had had for years, was further from him than he had ever been. While his body worked away at the task at hand, his mind continued to wander as it always did. He still thought of how the world would react to Vincent. How all would want to hear of his journey so far on earth. But he could not help but wonder had he waited too long, that perhaps he had missed his opportunity. Just then he was drawn back to reality as the men of the yard began to gather around a newspaper.

"Wow, what a waste! Would ya look at her!" spoke The Senator as he leaned on a yard brush and looked over Bobby's shoulder. "Jesus, I would have shown her a fine time."

Robert closed the paper and turned back in disgust at The Senator. "Jesus Christ, Damien, have you even one respectful bone in your body?"

"What, like," replied The Senator, "just because she's dead doesn't mean she wasn't good looking, like. Besides, me saying it doesn't change nothing. And another thing, *Robert*, don't call me Damien, I worked too hard for that nickname."

A few more of the men gathered around, John included. "What are ye guys talking about?"

The Senator began, "Some old doll was found dead, a young one too. Read it out there, Bobby." Robert opened up the front pages of the paper and began to read aloud.

"Gardaí, along with the help of Cork water rescue have recovered a body from the River Lee. The body was seen drifting among debris by Penrose Wharf yesterday morning by a woman walking on her way to work. The body is suspected to be that of missing persons Fiona O'Connor who was last seen leaving her work at The Upstairs nightclub off Liberty Street. However, these reports are as yet unconfirmed. Gardaí are treating the incident as suspicious…"

John could not believe his ears. "Let me see that!" He grabbed the paper from Robert's hands and fell into a daze as the men spoke around him. Others looked at her picture over John's shoulder and commented on how good-looking she was. John desperately scanned the rest of the article. One of the other men spoke. "Oh, Jesus, that's who ye're on about. One of the lads down at Kelly's Bar is a guard and he was sayin' that when they pulled her out of the water they said it looked as if her neck had been broken, but ah, he said not to be saying that around so you know, you didn't hear nothing from me, like."

John stayed standing there as the men went back to work. "Hold onto it, John, lad," spoke Robert. "I'm done with it anyway."

John said nothing as he started to walk away. He turned back to Robert and said, "Tell Tony that I had to go home early, that I'll, ah, that I'll make it up tomorrow. I have to go to… I just have to go."

228

Robert narrowed his eyes and shouted after John "Buddy, are ya all right? John, John, where are you going?"

John was going home to find out where Vincent had been two nights ago.

CHAPTER VII

EXODUS

And on the seventh day, man was created.

***

By the time John made it home it was dark. He had read the article over and over again the entire bus ride home. He even got off the bus early and ran the last mile. He could not wait. He had to know as soon as possible.

As he ran up the staircase of his building he shouted out for Vincent. He screamed his name as if he was already demanding an answer. A panicked John burst into an apartment that was dressed in an altogether more different tone. There was no sign of Vincent. Something was up, John couldn't put his finger on it, but something was up. He stood in the entrance of the flat, with the door swung wide as he called out for him, "Vincent! Vincent?"

And that was when he noticed it sitting there by the kitchen counter. There, tucked neatly against the worktop, sat a small brown suitcase. John had never seen it before. His face contorted as he looked upon the suitcase and tried to make sense of the situation when Vincent walked out of the bathroom.

"Hello, John." He spoke in a sombre tone. John was still playing catch-up on a number of topics.

"Vince, what the hell is – I mean – the newspaper... and that thing? Vince, what the hell is going on here?"

"I think it is more than obvious, John." John pointed down at the suitcase.

"What the hell is that thing and where did it come from?"

"You know very well what it is, John, I bought it in town today while you were at work."

"Vince, what's…"

"I'm leaving, John!" shouted Vincent before repeating softly, "I'm leaving." The rain had started to fall against the window of the bedroom.

John did not know where to begin. "Leaving? Leaving to go where, why?"

Vincent bent down and picked up his suitcase. "There is a hostel near the chipper that I'm going to rent for a short time and please, spare us both the question of why, the answer is too much for us both."

John walked past Vincent and took the case from his hand and put it back down on the ground.

"You can't leave, Vincent! Not like this, not after what you've done. What, what was going to happen? Did you think I would just come home and find that you were gone, that I'd just forget about you, like?"

"I wanted to be gone by the time you were back from work, yes. From how this is going I think you can see why, John."

John had lost his fear. He had lost his anger. All he felt was the crushing weight at the prospect of being alone. He felt hollow inside.

"But why?"

"Why, John, you want to know why?"

"Yeah, like why can't you stay here?"

"Why, because I've wasted too much time here already, John, that's why!"

Vincent's tone was beginning to seethe with hatred. He began to speak through his teeth.

"I hate it here, John! I hate it!"

John was shocked, he stood there open mouthed and broken hearted.

"I hate what you've done to me!"

"What *I've* done to *you?*"

"Yes, John, this is all your doing! You made me like this."

"Like what?"

"Weak and feeble, like you! What misfortune I had. Of all the houses I could have landed in, of all the places on Earth I could have fallen I end up with a failure like you."

John gritted his teeth. The heart break was replaced with anger. John narrowed his brow and shook his head.

"You know what, Vince, I was better off before I ever knew you."

"No you weren't, how could you have been worse when you were rock bottom? You would have been better off if I had landed right on top of you and killed you then and there. It would save you the misery of the next forty years. Me, I would have rather landed in that black, shitty river out there than this squalid hell that has been my prison.

"How fucking dare you! How dare you speak to me like that, Vince! I made you what you are!"

"Exactly, you moron! You made me into this!"

"No, no I didn't. I took care of you, I showed you how to live when all others would have taken advantage of you."

"You showed me how to *survive!* And get off of your pedestal, because you were plotting and planning how to take advantage of me every day since I got here. You would have done it just like anyone else except you were too stupid. Or pathetic, or both! And in all your hesitation you let me to rot!"

"I let you to rot? No, Vincent, this was your own doing. Your corruption was at your hands, it was your own doing."

"You did it to me, John, I was your responsibility and you led me astray. Brought me like a horse to water to all the temptations that have served in my ruin. The flavours I cannot help but taste. The mundane jobs of life. This, this place. No good can come to anyone living in a dark and depressing hole as is the one in which we scrounge from day to day, like rats."

"There is a lot worse out there, you pompous asshole."

"And there is a lot better, too, John, there is a lot better too. And I would die here a rotten mess having only read and dreamed of a world you were holding me back from."

"Holding you back? All I've ever done is look out for you, try to protect you."

Vincent shook his head as his eyes filled with tears of intense hatred.

"Protect me? John, you have done more damage to me than anyone else on this Earth."

John recoiled. "Ha, well, aren't you just perfect? Well, let he who is without sin…" John threw the crumpled newspaper at Vincent with all his force, "…cast the first stone!"

The pages danced around the air, as Vincent looked at John in utter confusion. "What the hell are you talking about, John?"

"You! You talk to me as if *I'm* the one who is causing damage here on Earth? What did you do with her, Vincent, what did you *do?*"

Vincent held out his hands and squinted without reply.

"Fiona, Vince, Fiona! What did you do to her?"

He stood there in silence. There was no answer.

"What did you…"

"I don't know what you're talking about!"

"No? No? Well maybe *this* will help remind you."

John found the story page with her photo and the article and pushed it against Vincent's chest.

"What is this?"

"Look at it!"

Vincent looked at the page, when he saw Fiona's picture his eyes grew wide. He then scanned the article.

"What do you want me to do with this?"

John was even more shocked than he expected. "That's it? That's all you have to say!"

"Well, what am I supposed to say, John?"

"That you're sorry! That you didn't do it!"

"Do it?"

"Don't play stupid, Vincent, I know you did it."

"Did what?"

"Killed her! You killed Fiona, Vincent."

"No I didn't, John! Ah don't be ridiculous, why would I kill her?"

John put his hands on his head. How his life had changed.

234

"You're not even surprised, Vince, you're not even surprised that she's in the newspaper. So don't do it, don't lie to me."

Vincent looked at the article one more time before he turned it over and put it face down on the counter. He turned to John.

"Now look. I'm sorry that she's dead, I am. But I had *nothing* to do with it. And if I am completely honest with you… I don't really care."

John backed away in disgust.

"What, John? Why should I? I haven't had anything to do with her in a long time; besides, there never really was anything to be done with her anyway. I had a crush on her and acted like a fool. She got rid of me and that was that. So I'm sorry if my heart doesn't bleed for her but I honestly don't care."

"She was *murdered*, Vince!" Vincent slapped a closed fist down on the counter.

"Jesus Christ, John, you just don't get it! I don't care!"

"But why, Vince, why…"

"Because I'm rotten inside, John, because my fire has gone out. Because I'm terrible and I'm awful and all the things that would make someone cold to the world as it is cold to them in turn. Besides, you don't know that she was murdered; the paper just says that she was found. That stupid bitch could have broken her neck when she fell into the river for all anyone knows."

He went to pick up his suitcase. John stuttered as he softly spoke.

"How… how did you know that?"

Vincent stopped mid motion.

"How did you know that her neck was broken, Vince?"

"Because it said in the article and…"

"No it didn't, it says nothing about that."

"Well, then I don't know, I mean I'm just guessing… from the sounds of it… like normally when people are found like that they… the water, it… I didn't do it, John. I didn't."

For the last time, both men were joined by the silence that all too often had filled the space between them. This time it was the loudest it had ever been. The tension was thick and dense and filled the room like an ether that hung heavy on their skin.

"I have to go now, John. Please, don't try and stop me."

"Stop you, why would I want to stop you? You know, I might be pathetic, I might be a failure but at least I'm not a monster."

Vincent stopped, his back turned to John.

"What did you say?" spoke Vincent coldly.

"You heard me. I'm not a monster, so at least I can be proud about that."

"Don't call me that, John. Take it back. Take it back right now before I leave."

"Why should I, Vince, it's the truth isn't it? You're a monster, a freak."

Vincent turned and boomed his voice at John as he shouted.

"Monster! Monster? I am a God among ants, John."

"No, you were, Vincent. Now you're just weak and feeble, like me, remember?"

Vincent laughed, "Clever, John, that's the most clever thing you've said the entire time I've known you. But I'm leaving now. And in a few minutes you'll be back exactly where you were, all alone."

He changed his tone to one of high pitched mockery, "*You and me, Vincent, you and me in the end*" he grinned at John, "No, John, in the end you will be alone. Me, when I get away from here, away from this place and away from you, I'll heal like I always do. And then my wings will get better and then I'll show everyone, then I'll show the whole world. And they'll love me, John. They'll adore me. They'll worship me. And in time to come, when I'm held high above them all, you'll undoubtedly crawl out from this very same, miserable rock you call home and say that you know me, and you'll tell them all about this time we had together. And I will spit down upon you like the stranger you will be. And no one, not one person will believe you. In the end, John, it will just be *me* and me alone."

He smiled as he turned on his heels. John was choking on emotion. He started:

"Yeah, well we'll see how far you get with other people, we'll see how they treat you." John lunged forward, "we'll see how far you get without my coat on your back, covering up what you really are!" John grabbed Vincent by the back of the coat and pulled at it sharply and desperately. It tugged at him and only came half off of his shoulders. Vince stumbled backwards and tripped over the suitcase. His lightning reflexes were no more. As he fell towards the ground his arms flailed in the air as the coat fanned and rippled at the bottom. To save his balance his wings too began to spread beneath the coat, but it was no use. He fell backwards. One of his wings touched the ground first and all of his weight came crashing down upon it

237

causing it to fold over on itself. There was a tremendous crack as the main stalk of his right wing shattered and snapped in half. Vincent spat and gargled in pain as he lay writhing on the floor. John was terrified. Vincent rolled over onto his side among a chorus of breaking bones. When he was sideways he vomited all over the floor. A pool of blood began to swell beneath him. It stank and the smell of the blood was hot in John's nostrils. He motioned to help Vincent up but he was batted away.

Vincent brought himself to his feet. He grimaced in pain while he struggled to remove the coat. He roared as his arms streamed like liquid from the sleeves. The coat fell next to the blood that was still spreading slowly across the floor. John picked up the coat and looked at the floor, there was such a large pool of blood, unusually large, it had spread far out across the floor and it was unusually thick. Lines ran across the blood and John could not figure out why. It was because the blood was draining through the floorboards. And then the blood began to thicken and it turned black. It was not a deep red, but pure black. John looked at it while Vincent struggled with his wing. In a matter of seconds it began to dry and crack, it looked like tar had been poured in the centre of the room. But John's focus was soon stolen. He looked upon Vincent's wings. It was the first time he had seen them in almost two months and he could scarcely believe his eyes.

"How bad... ah... how bad is it, John?" asked Vincent in a panic he had never breathed before. John did not answer as he was still absorbed by shock.

Where there had once been glorious wings of pristine white there were two shrivelled stalks. They were contorted and looked as though they were after shrinking. They were almost completely bare of feathers, just a few on either wing remained. They were raggedy and bony and John struggled to look at them because they frightened him, they were the starkest reality he had seen in a long time. Those wings, shrivelled and deformed, finally burst his bubble and made what had happened, what *was* happening, all too real.

"John!" Vincent shouted as he struggled to look over his shoulder, "How bad is it?"

It was bad. The wing was snapped about two-thirds of the length down and the skin was torn and ripped all around it. Below the breaking point, the wing was limp and looked like a balloon that had been deflated.

"John! Answer me!"

"It's pretty bad, Vince, it's…I'm sorry, I didn't mean to do this."

"Sorry? You're sorry! Is it bleeding?"

"No, it looks like it's stopped."

"Good, now hand me my coat."

"No."

"What? John, give me my coat."

"No, Vincent, I'm sorry, but this, that, it doesn't change anything. Like you said. You'll heal, like you always do. If you're going to go then go, but you're not getting my help anymore. Nothing, not even that coat and besides, it's my coat."

"John, stop being petty and give me back the coat."

"No, Vincent, just leave. We'll see what kind of god they hail you as now."

Vincent walked towards John, he stepped on what was the pool of blood, it shattered and cracked beneath his foot like a disc of glass. But there was no time for that as he advanced towards John.

"I mean it, Vince, just turn around and…"

Vincent grabbed him by the throat and began to lift him off the ground. John grabbed at his wrists and scrawled them. Vincent pulled him close to his face. How greatly he had aged. It was as if the blood that had left his wings was the last drop of divinity in his body. His face was so grey and weathered, up close John could see the chippings and discolouration of his teeth and his eyes, his eyes were almost completely black, only a thin rim of grey-blue remained. He was wheezing in pain and exhaustion as he held John in the air.

"I'm not *asking*, John, I'm *telling*. Now I'm going to take my coat and leave."

With that he raised John up high once more and slammed him down through the coffee table that sat in the middle of the room and reached for his coat.

But he struggled with it; his wing was causing him more trouble than he wanted to admit. Outside the storm was raging against the glass. John lay wheezing on the floor. He had nothing left to lose.

"Is it because she said no? Was that it?" Vincent paid him no attention. John repeated his question louder.

"Is it because she said no?" Vincent, while clearly agitated replied to John.

"What are you talking about?"

"Fiona, that's why you killed her, because she said no."

John managed to sit himself upright among the wooden debris and laughed once or twice.

"How did it happen, did you wait for her outside work, huh? Or did ya follow her, like a weirdo. I bet you followed her."

Vincent's face began to wrinkle around his nose; he turned away from John and tried to pretend he was not listening. He wanted to get the trench coat on over his back and be gone from the place. The lightning had begun outside and the air was alive with distant thunder growing ever closer. John made his way to his feet and continued to laugh.

"Ha-ha I bet that was it. Ha, I've got it now. I bet you decided to leave me and thought to yourself that you could get Fiona to run away with you! But you haven't been having the luck with the worst of them lately, have ya? Let alone the types that look like Fiona, well, what she used to look like."

John hobbled over to the doorway of the bedroom and continued: "How did you ask her, Vince, what did you say? I bet you sounded like a NUT! I'd say you even begged her too."

Vincent stopped fumbling with the coat and turned to look at John who was lost in his own words. He rattled sentence after sentence from his lips as the realisations continued to flood free to his brain.

"Oh my God, I bet that, I bet that that you got so desperate to convince her to come that you… you did, you told her didn't you? You told her the truth about you. I bet you probably even showed her those, those deformities on your back!"

John slapped his face as he laughed even though he knew there was nothing funny between them.

"Oh my God you did. To think of it, the poor girl. How frightened she must have been. How scared you must have been when she tried to run. And that must have been when you did it. That was why you killed her. She died because she knew and she wouldn't come away with you. And you think everyone will be different. Go on take the coat, you need it, you need all the help you can get. That poor girl."

Vincent went to protest his innocence in rage when John cut across him.

"Oh my God, you're right, Vincent, you're right. I have made you just like me. You're like me because you're all alone. Ha-ha, oh my, you are all alone!" John started to lean against the doorframe as he laughed. He had finally come to terms with his own failure and took solace in the fact that if a creature as magnificent as Vincent had succumbed to the same fate, then maybe he wasn't so pathetic after all. Like men so often do, they drag others down to their depths. Misery loves company just as failure loves a friend. John continued to taunt Vincent with the truth.

"You think that by leaving this place that you're making things better, that things will change for you. But don't you see it? Don't you see the irony? By you leaving, ha-ha, by you leaving it's actually you *yourself* making you into me. The second you walk out that door you're all alone. So don't you see! You can't go! And you can't stay here! You have no choice! An outcast. They didn't want you up there..." John pointed upwards and out towards his window, towards the sky and the storm, "...and no one wants you down here. So go on, get out! And make sure to wave when you 'spit down on top of me.'"

John's laughter trailed off. Vincent had dropped the coat and instead held two solid fists, his fingers clenched tight. John looked at him and said in his most spiteful tone: "Behold, Gabriel, the loneliest monster of them all."

Vincent walked a heavy pace at John and both men snarled their faces. Vincent threw a fist, which sent John stumbling backwards into his room as his fist made contact with his face. John stumbled back and fell against his bedside locker. Vincent went to punch him again but John dived onto the bed, Vincent's fist instead went through the glass. The cold storm howled as it bled into the room. John scrambled in fear on the bed with nowhere to go. Feathers were flying and turning to rust coloured dust in the air. Vincent grabbed him by the back and dragged him onto the ground. The bed sheets, pillows and a worn copy of 'Riddle of the Sands' fell to the floorboards.

Vincent crouched down and started punching John who was resting against the frame of the bed. Each punch was tremendous but John struggled in defense. John's hands scrambled around Vincent's back. He managed to get hold of his broken wing. He squeezed it tight and began to twist it as hard as he could. Vincent shrieked out in pain as more of the few feathers fell from his back. The room was dark and John's eyes were swollen and filled with blood; he could barely see what he was doing. But the lightning that came in through the hole in the glass illuminated the room in terrible flashes. He put all his energy into the reaches of his arms and twisted the wing as hard as he could. Vincent released his grasp as he reached behind in agony to desperately free his wings.

John took the advantage and began to crawl for the door. But it was no use. Weakened though Vincent was, he was still far greater in strength than most men on earth ever were. He was still much more powerful than John. He cast the pain aside and exchanged it for rage as he reached out and grabbed John by the ankles. He dragged him back towards him and fell down atop him. Both men struggled on the floor. Eventually, Vincent flipped John over to look at him. He began to beat him ferociously until his face was pulp beneath his knuckles. He screamed at him and howled above the wind outside. The orange streetlamp began to flicker until it eventually buzzed and clinked out. Now the room was only in light with the night time blue and the blackness of the ill-lit blood.

Vincent leaned on John as he panted, exhausted from beating his friend. He slowly wrapped his massive hands around his neck as John gurgled and spat. Vincent began to close his fingers around John's neck as he spoke.

"You and me in the end, *buddy*. You and me. Well, John, I guess you were right." His nails began to pierce the skin of his neck. John's fingers desperately danced as they skipped from trying to pry the fingers free from his throat and grab at Vincent's face. Vincent leaned back to escape the reach of John and continued to talk.

"The loneliest monster, huh? Well, if I'm such a lonely monster then how come I'm not alone? Well? Aren't I here with my *best* pal..." he squeezed even tighter, John's eyes felt as though they would burst.

"... My best pal. But if I'm going to be..." John struggled the last he could struggle, "...a lonely monster, then I have to be all alone, don't I? Don't I!" Vincent shouted as he began to cry. He released his grasp around John's neck and grabbed him by his face. Vincent leaned into John as he pulled his face towards him.

"You and me in the end, John, you and me in the end." With that the last of the lightning lit the sky as he slammed John's head into the floorboards and burst the back of his skull clean open. The storm stopped suddenly outside. It was gone and so was John.

He lay there, limp on the bedroom floor. The blood drained from his head and ran into the scorched lines of wood that Vincent had made the first night he crashed into that room, the lines he made as he lay roasting on the ground. John's blood filled the veins of scorched wood as he lay cold in the very same spot. Vincent began to cry and wheeze like he had never done before. He called out desperately for John, asking him to get up, to wake up. He apologized as he held him close and cried.

He told him he was sorry, that he didn't want to be alone. The last feather fell from his wings and dissolved into dust in the growing pool of John's blood. Vincent now knew the very meaning of mortality as he held his only friend in his arms.

Despite his best plans and despite his biggest fears, he was alone. Who would mind him now? Who could he trust with his secret, and would anyone believe him? In John he lost all that he ever was. In John he lost himself.

It was never meant to end like this; it never had a chance of being any other way. There is no escaping the gravity of this Earth.